Disney Fairies

Tinker Bell and the Flying Monster

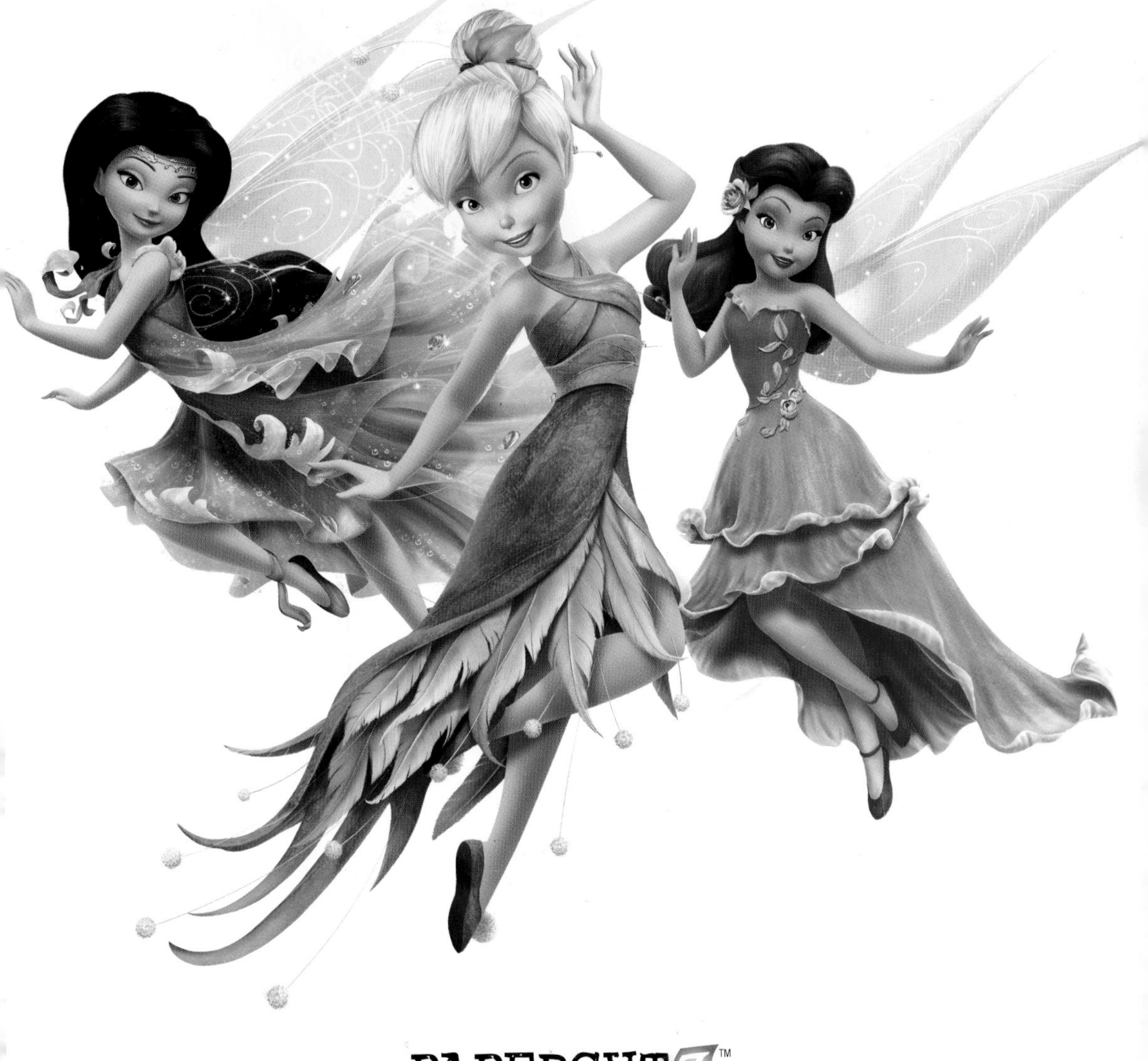

PAPERCUTZ™

Graphic Novels Available from
PAPERCUTZ

Graphic Novel #1
"Prilla's Talent"

Graphic Novel #2
"Tinker Bell and the
Wings of Rani"

Graphic Novel #3
"Tinker Bell and the
Day of the Dragon"

Graphic Novel #4
"Tinker Bell
to the Rescue"

Graphic Novel #5
"Tinker Bell and the
Pirate Adventure"

Graphic Novel #6
"A Present
for Tinker Bell"

Graphic Novel #7
"Tinker Bell the
Perfect Fairy"

Graphic Novel #8
"Tinker Bell and her
Stories for a Rainy Day"

Graphic Novel #9
"Tinker Bell and
her Magical Arrival"

Graphic Novel #10
"Tinker Bell and
the Lucky Rainbow"

Graphic Novel #11
"Tinker Bell and the
Most Precious Gift"

Graphic Novel #12
"Tinker Bell and the
Lost Treasure"

Graphic Novel #13
"Tinker Bell and the
Pixie Hollow Games"

Graphic Novel #14
"Tinker Bell and
Blaze"

Graphic Novel #15
"Tinker Bell and the
Secret of the Wings"

Graphic Novel #16
"Tinker Bell and the
Pirate Fairy"

Graphic Novel #17
"Tinker Bell and the
Legend of the NeverBeast"

Graphic Novel #18
"Tinker Bell and her
Magical Friends"

Graphic Novel #19
"Tinker Bell and the
Flying Monster"

**Tinker Bell
and the Great
Fairy Rescue**

DISNEY FAIRIES graphic novels are available in paperback for $7.99 each; in hardcover for $12.99 each except #5, $6.99PB, $10.99HC. #6-14 are $7.99PB $11.99HC. #15 – 18 are $7.99PB $12.99HC. #19 is $7.99PB $13.99HC. Tinker Bell and the Great Fairy Rescue is $9.99 in hardcover only.
Available at booksellers everywhere.

See more at papercutz.com

Or you can order from us: Please add $4.00 for postage and handling for first book, and add $1.00 for each additional book.
Please make check payable to NBM Publishing. Send to: Papercutz, 160 Broadway, Suite 700, East Wing, New York, NY 10038
or call 800 886 1223 (9-6 EST M-F) MC-Visa-Amex accepted.

Disney FAIRIES

#19 "Tinker Bell and the Flying Monster"

Contents

PAPERCUTZ™

NEW YORK

Disney Fairies #19
"Tinker Bell and the Flying Monster"

"The Flying Monster"
Script: Silvia Lombardi
Layout: Veronica Di Lorenzo
Inks: Santa Zangari
Cleanup: Rosa La Barbera
Color: Studio Kawaii

"Snail Trail"
Script: Silvia Lombardi
Layout: Sara Storino
Inks: Santa Zangari
Cleanup: Veronica Di Lorenzo
Color: Studio Kawaii

"Musical Beads"
Script: Silvia Lombardi
Layout: Nicola Sanmarco
Inks: Santa Zangari
Cleanup: Rosa La Barbera
Color: Studio Kawaii

"A Nice Misunderstanding"
Script: Tea Orsi
Layout: Giada Perissinotto
Inks: Santa Zangari
Cleanup: Miriam Gambino
Color: Studio Kawaii

"Up To Ten"
Script: Tea Orsi
Layout: Emilio Urbano
Inks: Santa Zangari
Cleanup: Rosa La Barbera
Color: Studio Kawaii

"The Love Letter"
Script: Tea Orsi
Layout: Marino Gentile
Inks: Santa Zangari
Cleanup: Miriam Gambino
Color: Studio Kawaii

"A Deep Down Talent"
Script: Tea Orsi
Layout: Nicola Sammarco
Inks: Santa Zangari
Cleanup: Letizia Algeri
Color: Studio Kawaii

"A Mysterious Trap"
Script: Tea Orsi
Layout: Marino Gentile
Inks: Santa Zangari
Cleanup: Veronica Di Lorenzo
Color: Studio Kawaii

"Fairy Self Control"
Script: Tea Orsi
Layout and Cleanup: Marino Gentile
Inks: Santa Zangari
Color: Studio Kawaii

"A Fuzzy Friend"
Script: Tea Orsi
Layout and Cleanup: Marino Gentile
Inks: Santa Zangari
Color: Studio Kawaii

"The Treasure Hunt"
Script: Tea Orsi
Layout and Cleanup: Sara Storino
Inks: Roberta Zanotta
Color: Studio Kawaii

"Nuts for Beauty"
Script: Silvia Lombard
Layout and Cleanup: Gianluca Barone
Inks: Santa Zangari
Color: Studio Kawaii

"Pirate Funfair"
Script: Silvia Lombard
Layout and Cleanup: Gianluca Barone
Inks: Santa Zangari
Color: Studio Kawaii

Minnie & Daisy #1 Preview -
"Much Ado About Juliet"
Script: Valentina Camerini
Layout: Gianluca Panniello
Inks: Cristina Giorgilli
Color: Dario Calabria
Graphic Illustrations: Gianluca Panniello

Papercutz books may be purchased for business or promotional use. For information on bulk purchases please contact Macmillan Corporate and Premium Sales Department at (800) 221-7945 x5442.

Production – Dawn Guzzo
Production Coordinator – Rachel Pinnelas
Editor – Robert V. Conte
Assistant Managing Editor – Jeff Whitman
Special Thanks to – Carlotta Quattrocolo, Arianna Marchione, Krista Wong, Eugene Paraszczuk
Jim Salicrup
Editor-in-Chief

ISBN: 978-1-62991-605-7 Paperback Edition
ISBN: 978-1-62991-606-4 Hardcover Edition

Printed in Korea
December 2016 through Four Color Print Group

Distributed by Macmillan
First Papercutz Printing

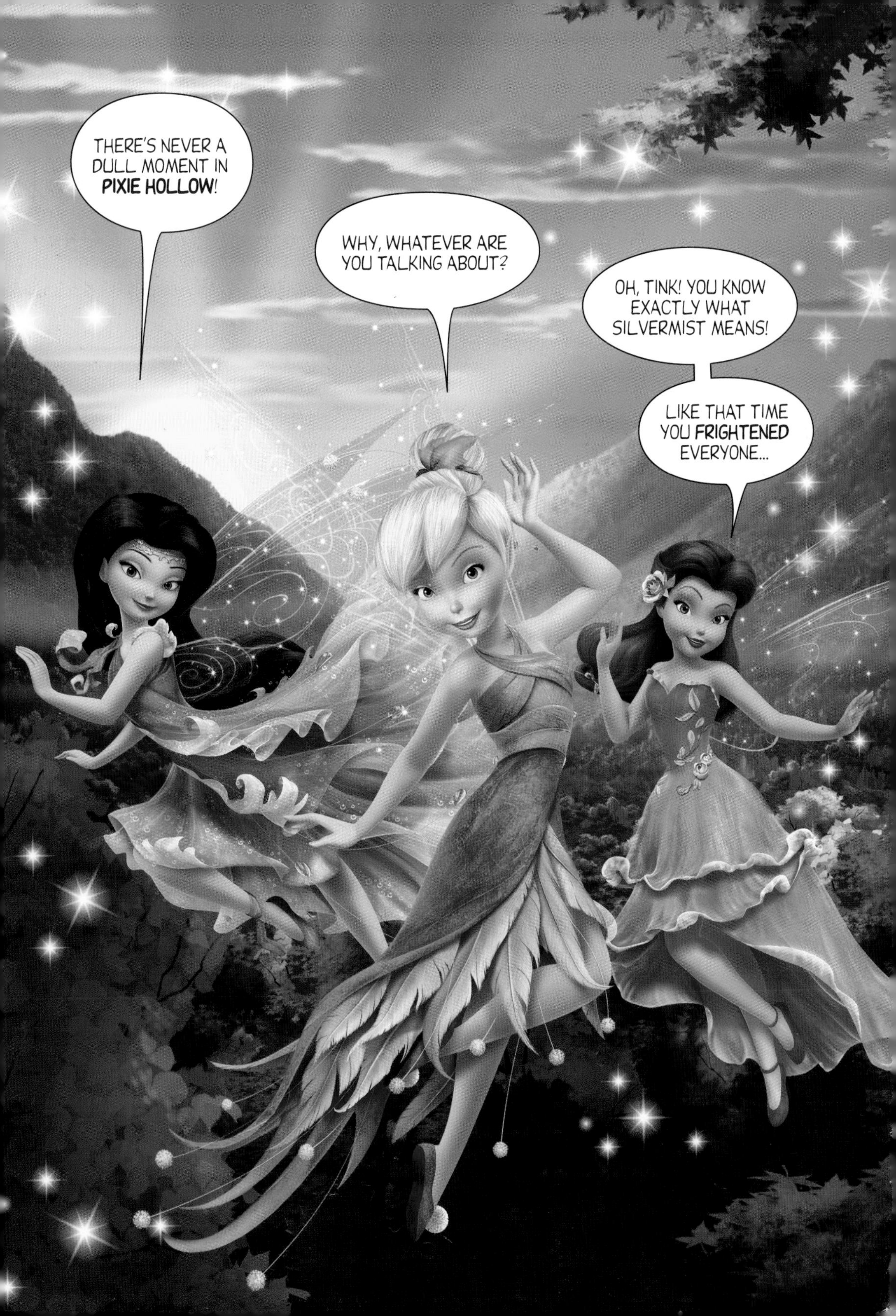
THERE'S NEVER A DULL MOMENT IN **PIXIE HOLLOW**!
WHY, WHATEVER ARE YOU TALKING ABOUT?
OH, TINK! YOU KNOW EXACTLY WHAT SILVERMIST MEANS!
LIKE THAT TIME YOU **FRIGHTENED** EVERYONE...

The Flying Monster

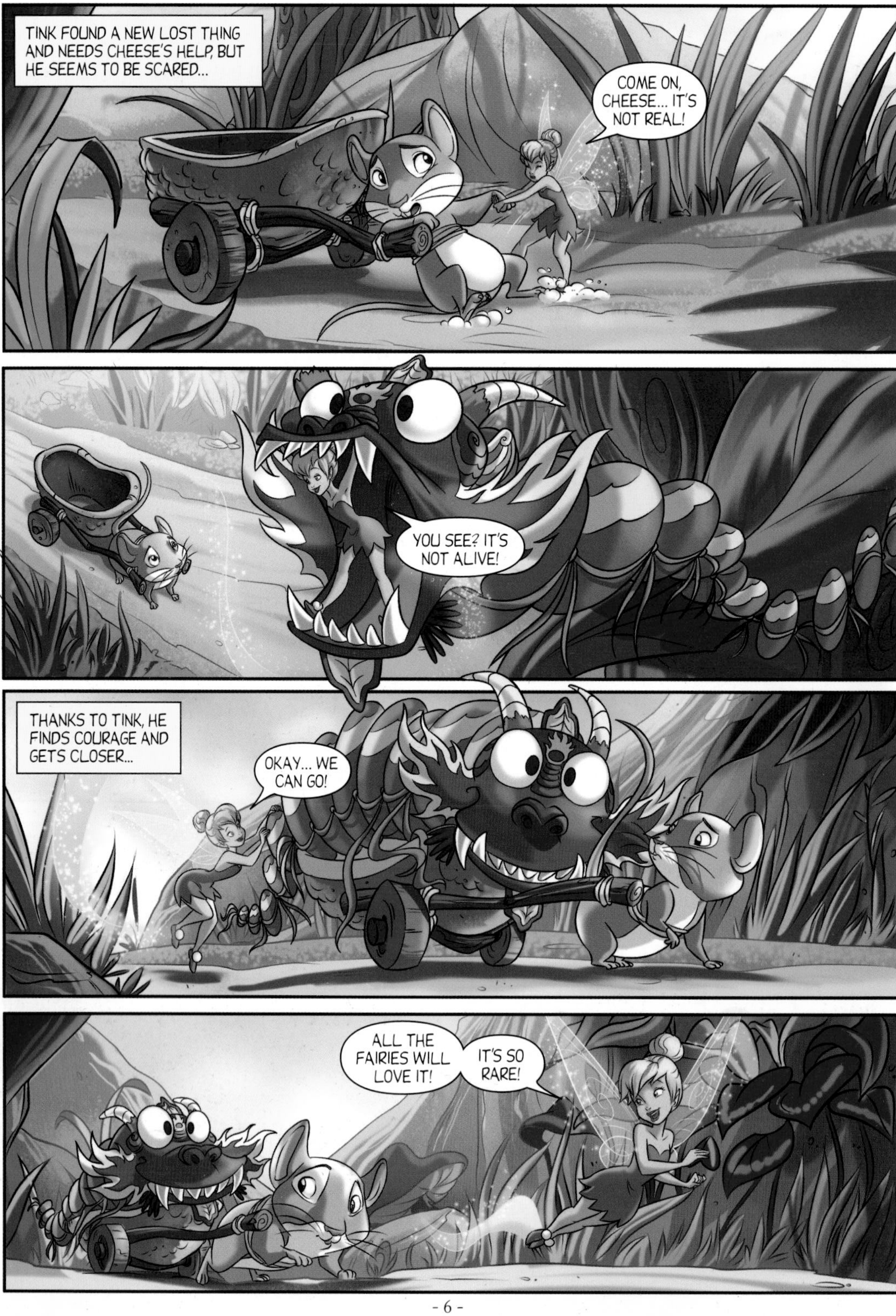
TINK FOUND A NEW LOST THING AND NEEDS CHEESE'S HELP, BUT HE SEEMS TO BE SCARED...
COME ON, CHEESE... IT'S NOT REAL!
YOU SEE? IT'S NOT ALIVE!
THANKS TO TINK, HE FINDS COURAGE AND GETS CLOSER...
OKAY... WE CAN GO!
ALL THE FAIRIES WILL LOVE IT!
IT'S SO RARE!

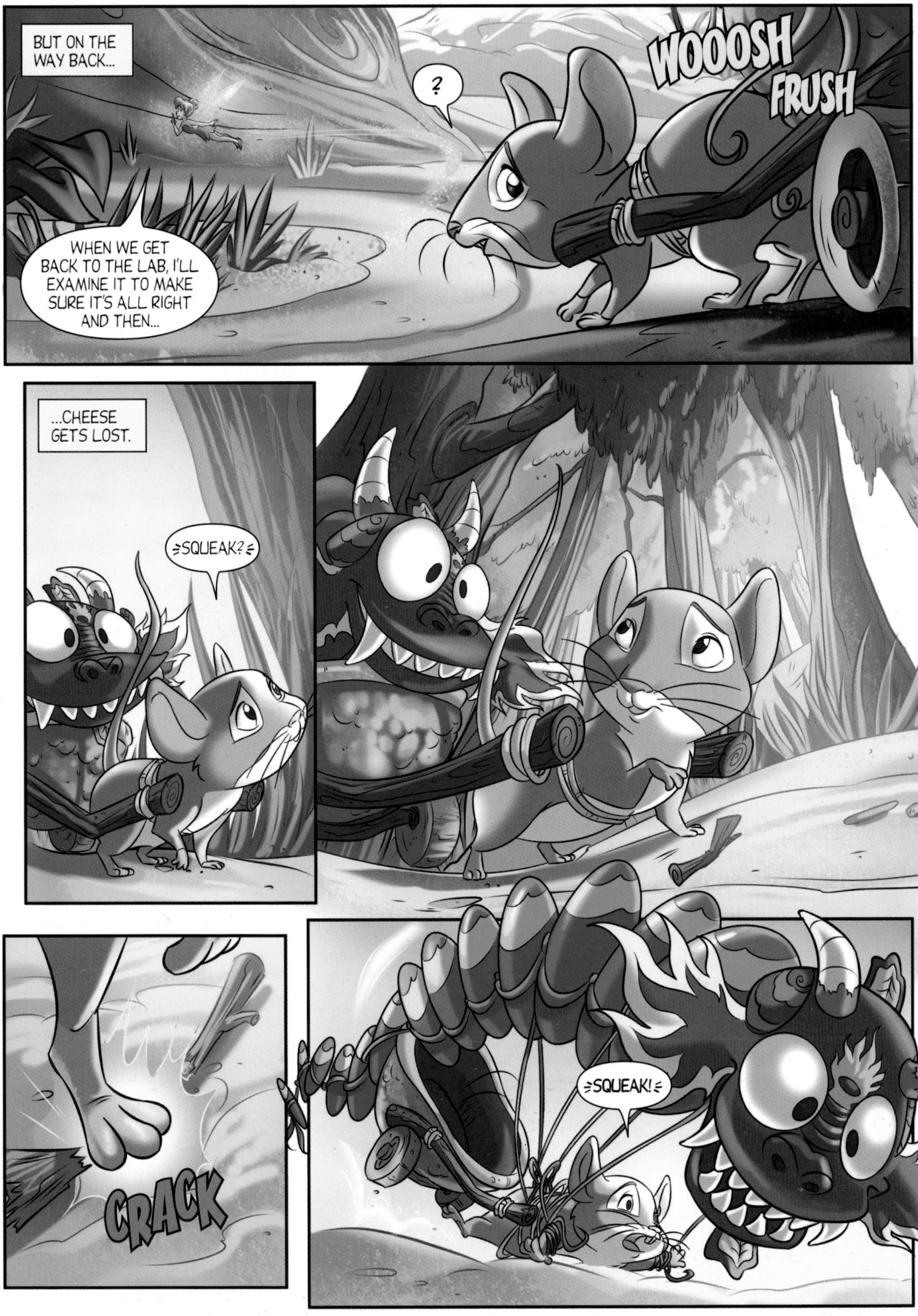
BUT ON THE WAY BACK...
?
WOOOSH
FRUSH
WHEN WE GET BACK TO THE LAB, I'LL EXAMINE IT TO MAKE SURE IT'S ALL RIGHT AND THEN...
...CHEESE GETS LOST.
SQUEAK?
CRACK
SQUEAK!

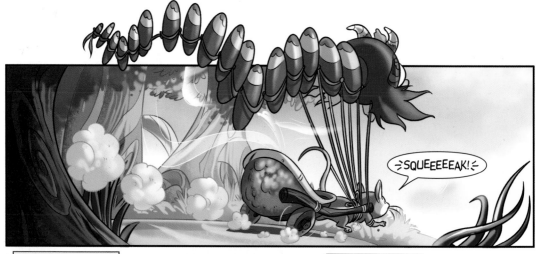

~SQUEEEEEAK!~

MEANWHILE, TINK HAS ARRIVED AT THE LAB...

CHEESE?

...AND REALIZES CHEESE IS MISSING!

CHEESE?

BUT THERE'S SOMETHING ELSE WRONG: ALL THE FAIRIES ARE FLYING AWAY!

HURRY UP! IT'S COMING!

DID YOU SEE CHEESE?

NO...

WHAT'S COMING?

WE DON'T KNOW WHAT IT IS, BUT IT'S TERRIFYING!

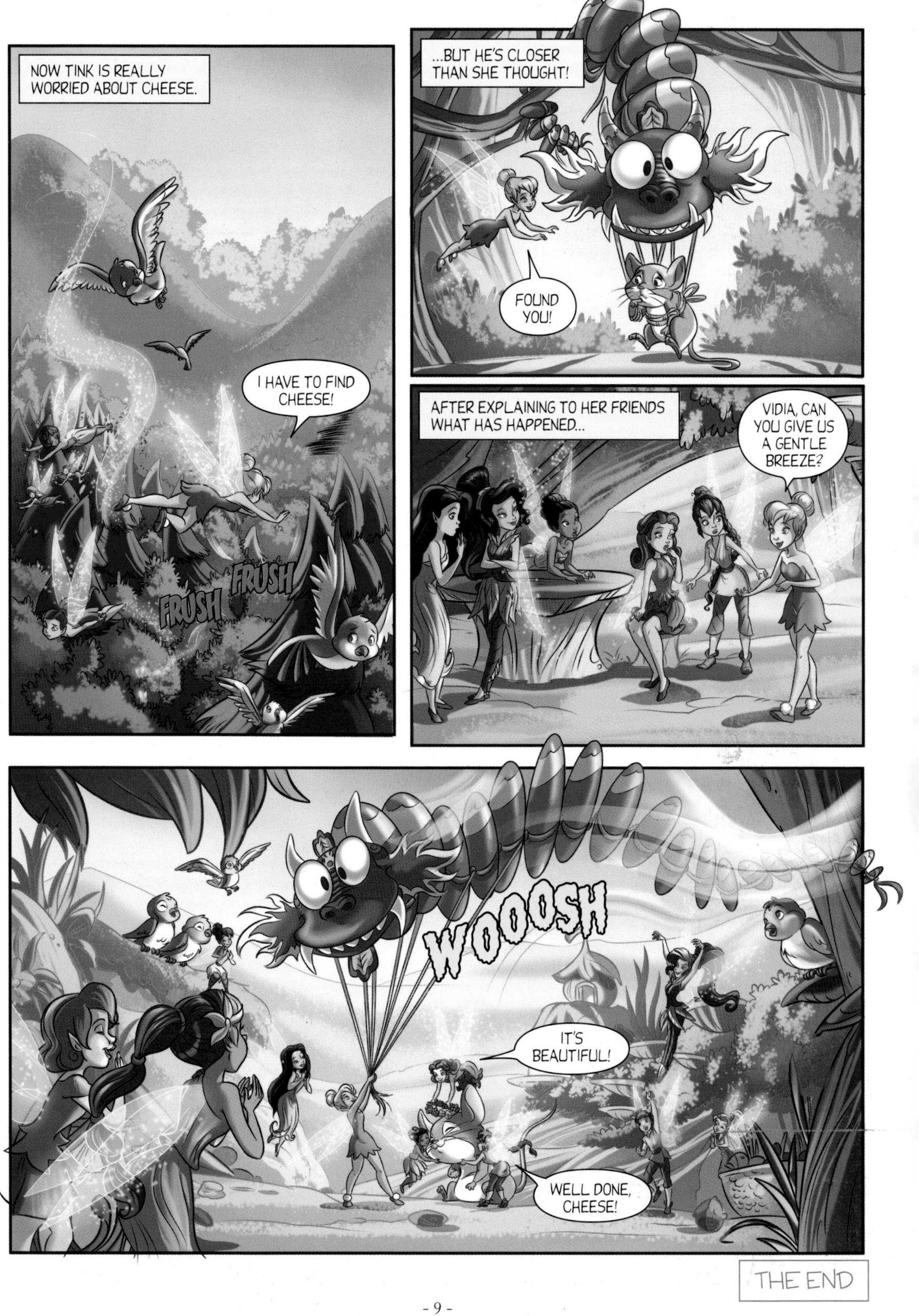
NOW TINK IS REALLY WORRIED ABOUT CHEESE.
I HAVE TO FIND CHEESE!
FRUSH
FRUSH
...BUT HE'S CLOSER THAN SHE THOUGHT!
FOUND YOU!
AFTER EXPLAINING TO HER FRIENDS WHAT HAS HAPPENED...
VIDIA, CAN YOU GIVE US A GENTLE BREEZE?
WOOOSH
IT'S BEAUTIFUL!
WELL DONE, CHEESE!

THE END

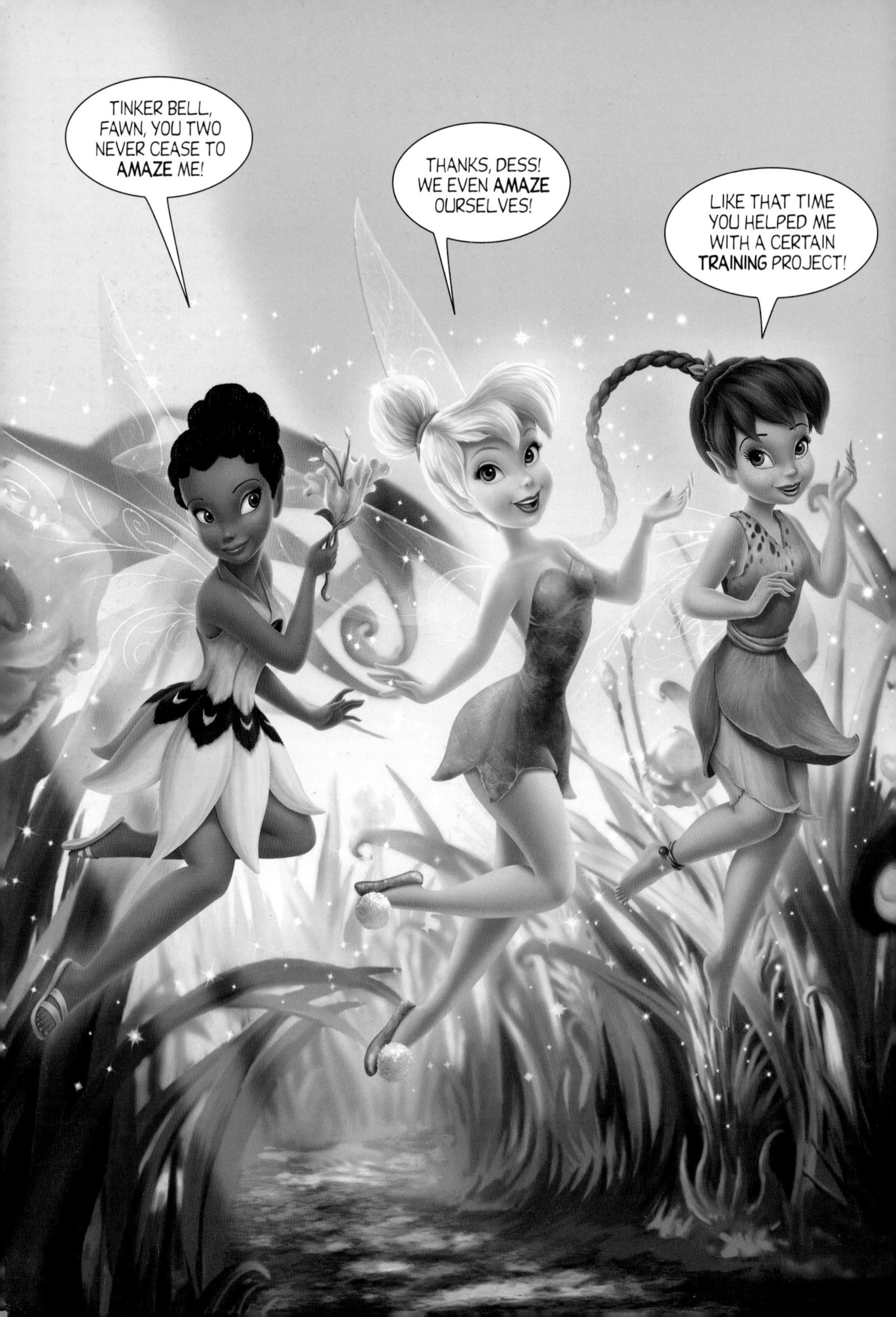
TINKER BELL, FAWN, YOU TWO NEVER CEASE TO AMAZE ME!
THANKS, DESS! WE EVEN AMAZE OURSELVES!
LIKE THAT TIME YOU HELPED ME WITH A CERTAIN TRAINING PROJECT!

Snail Trail

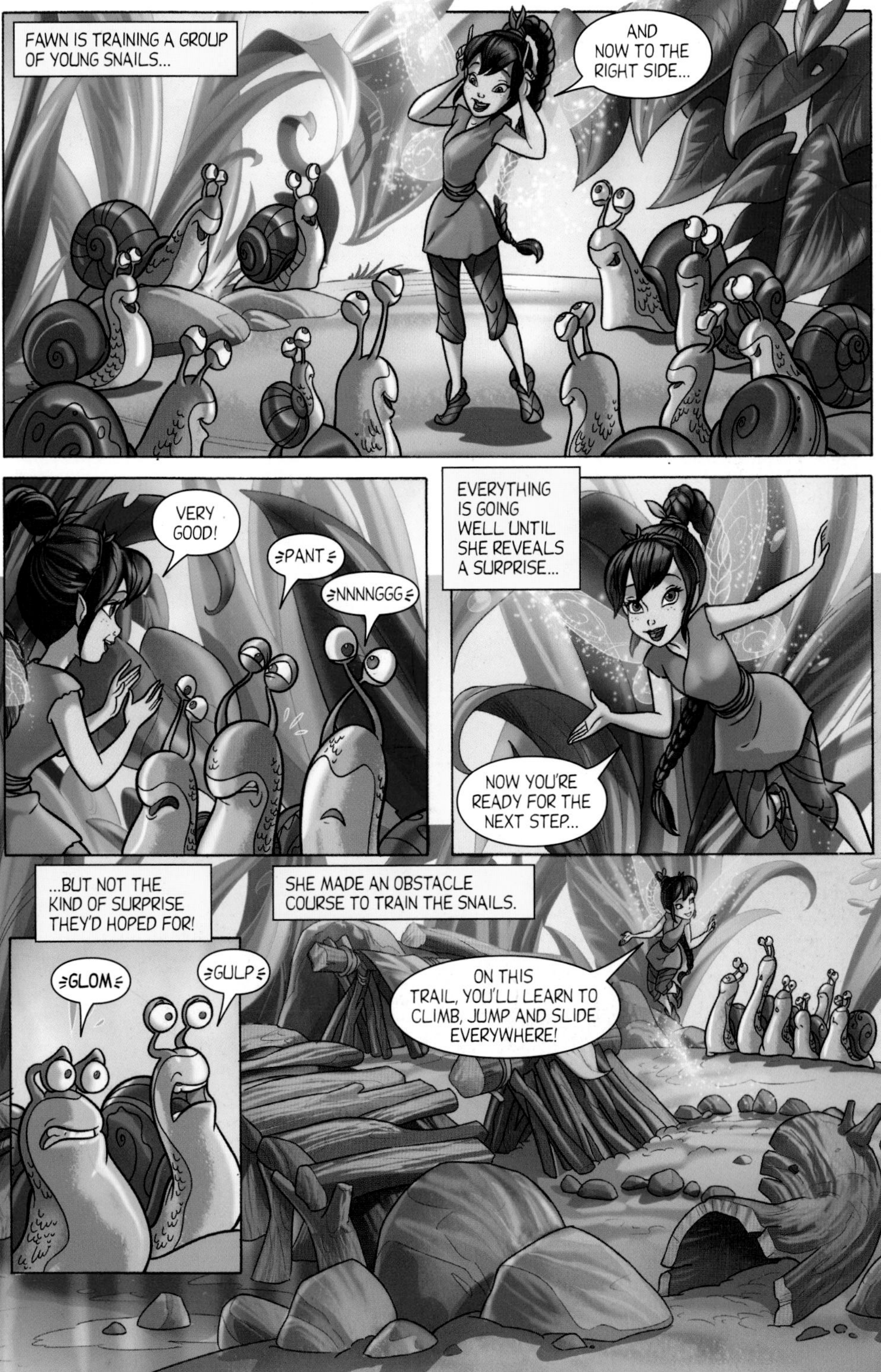

FAWN IS TRAINING A GROUP OF YOUNG SNAILS...
AND NOW TO THE RIGHT SIDE...
VERY GOOD!
PANT
NNNNGGG
EVERYTHING IS GOING WELL UNTIL SHE REVEALS A SURPRISE...
NOW YOU'RE READY FOR THE NEXT STEP...
...BUT NOT THE KIND OF SURPRISE THEY'D HOPED FOR!
GLOM
GULP
SHE MADE AN OBSTACLE COURSE TO TRAIN THE SNAILS.
ON THIS TRAIL, YOU'LL LEARN TO CLIMB, JUMP AND SLIDE EVERYWHERE!

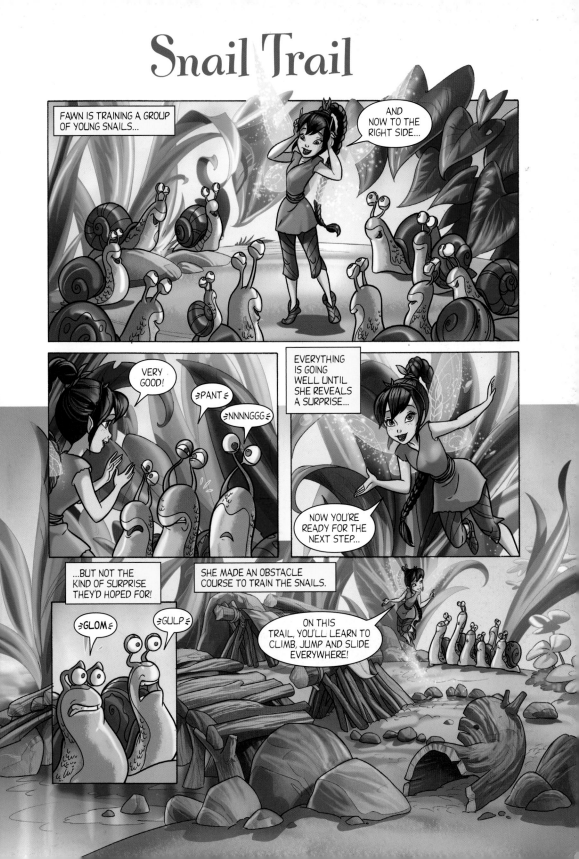

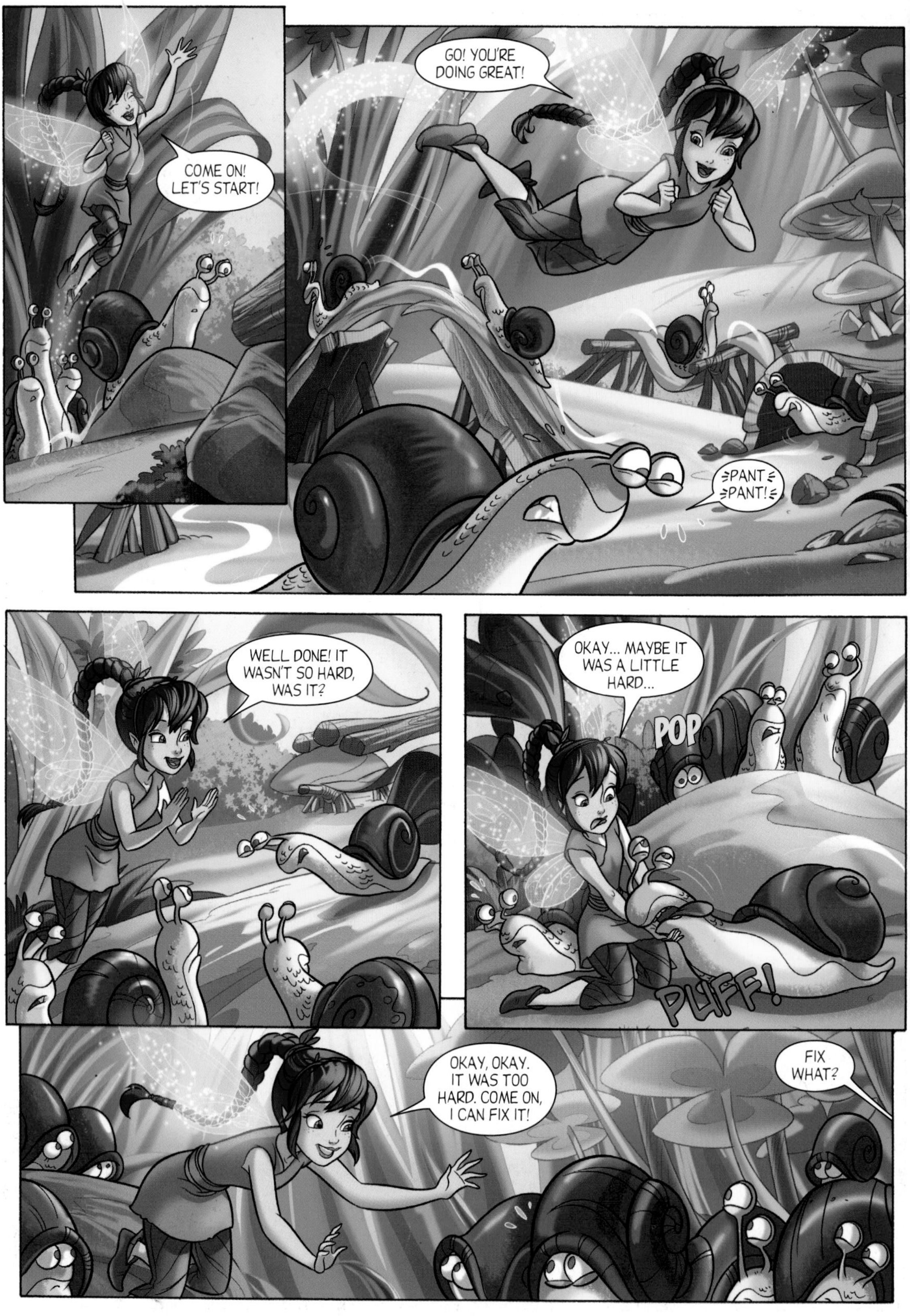
COME ON! LET'S START!
GO! YOU'RE DOING GREAT!
PANT PANT!
WELL DONE! IT WASN'T SO HARD, WAS IT?
OKAY... MAYBE IT WAS A LITTLE HARD...
POP
PUFF!
OKAY, OKAY. IT WAS TOO HARD. COME ON, I CAN FIX IT!
FIX WHAT?

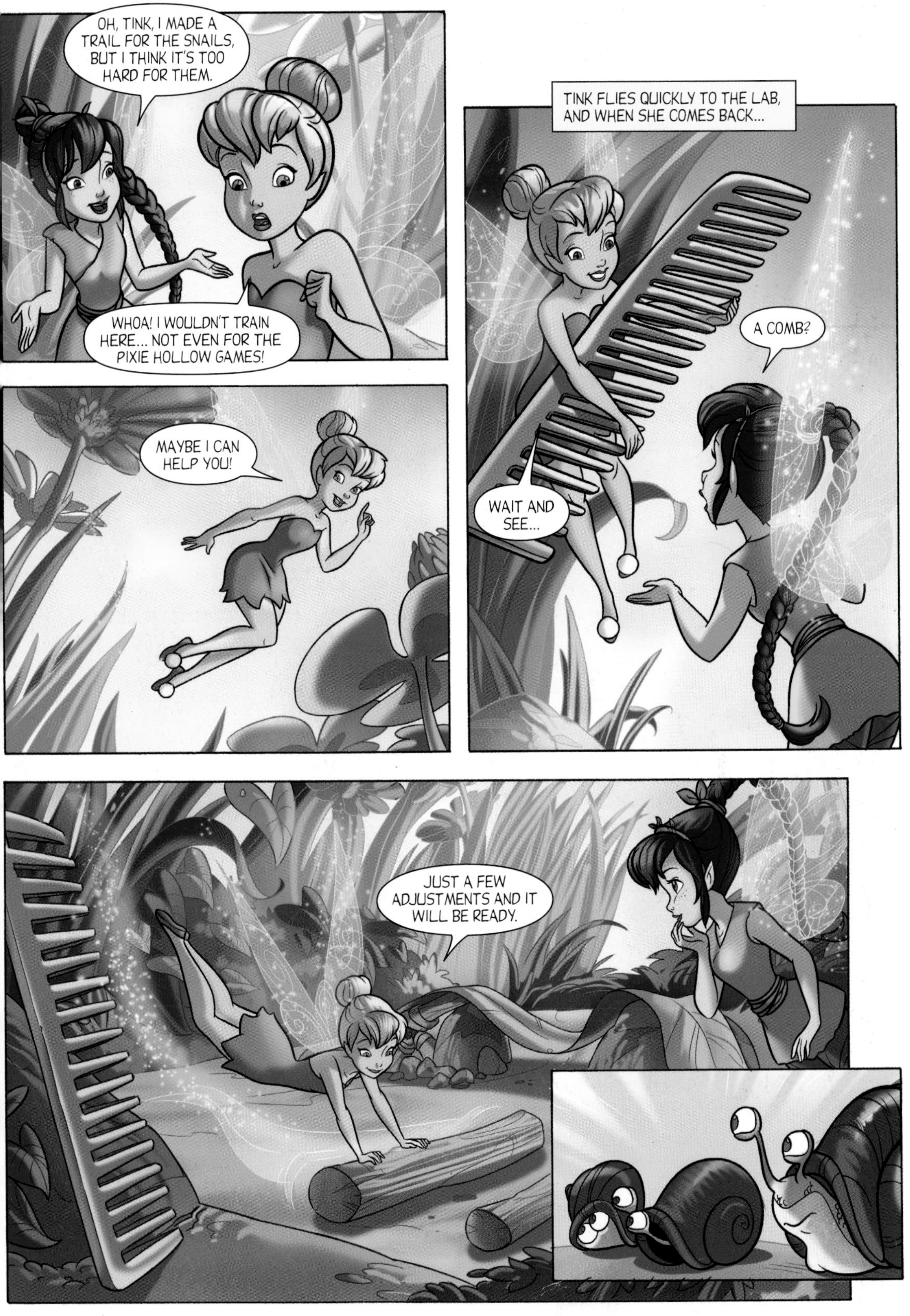
OH, TINK, I MADE A TRAIL FOR THE SNAILS, BUT I THINK IT'S TOO HARD FOR THEM.
WHOA! I WOULDN'T TRAIN HERE... NOT EVEN FOR THE PIXIE HOLLOW GAMES!
MAYBE I CAN HELP YOU!
TINK FLIES QUICKLY TO THE LAB, AND WHEN SHE COMES BACK...
A COMB?
WAIT AND SEE...
JUST A FEW ADJUSTMENTS AND IT WILL BE READY.

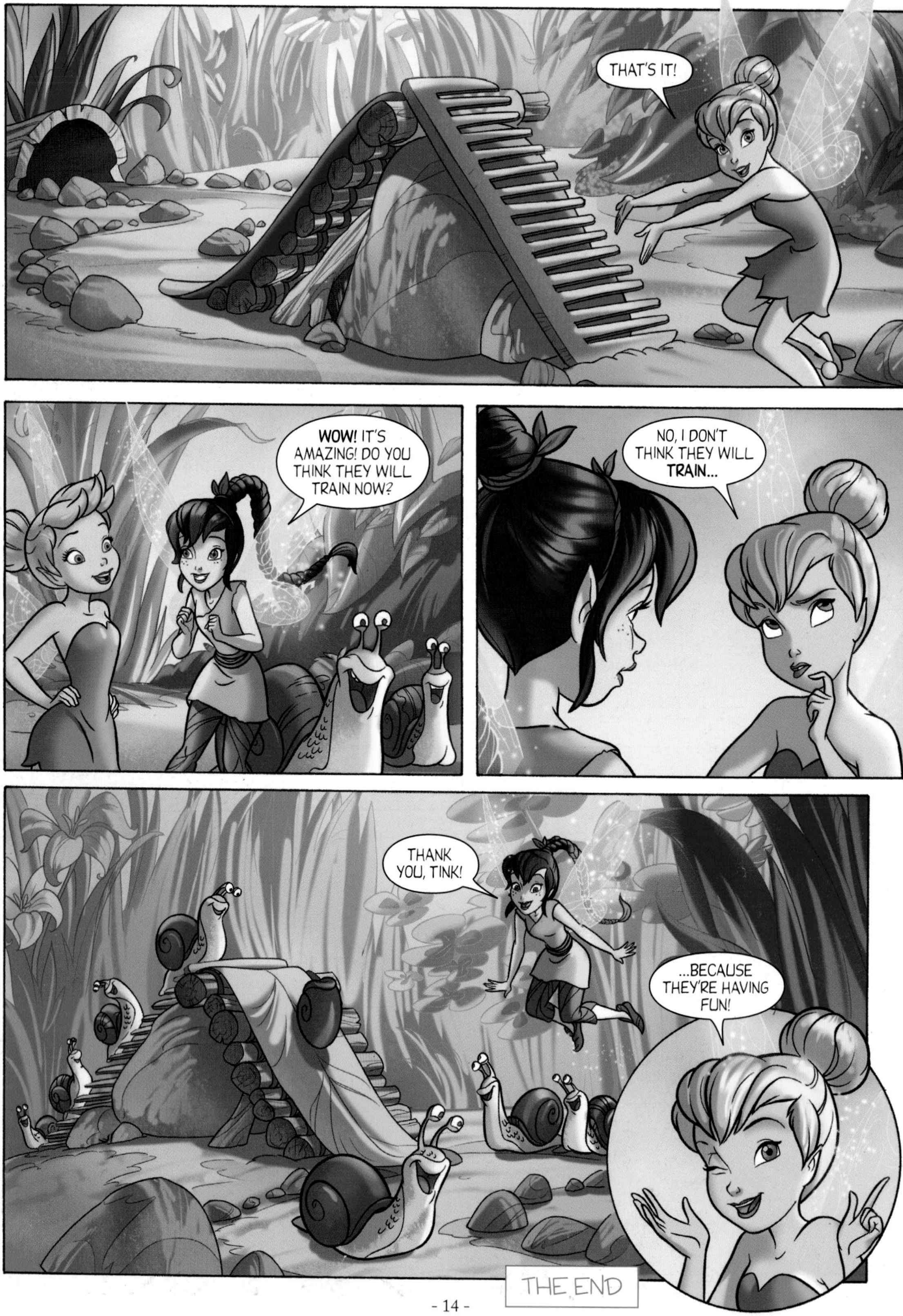
THAT'S IT!
WOW! IT'S AMAZING! DO YOU THINK THEY WILL TRAIN NOW?
NO, I DON'T THINK THEY WILL **TRAIN...**
THANK YOU, TINK!
...BECAUSE THEY'RE HAVING FUN!
THE END

Musical Beads

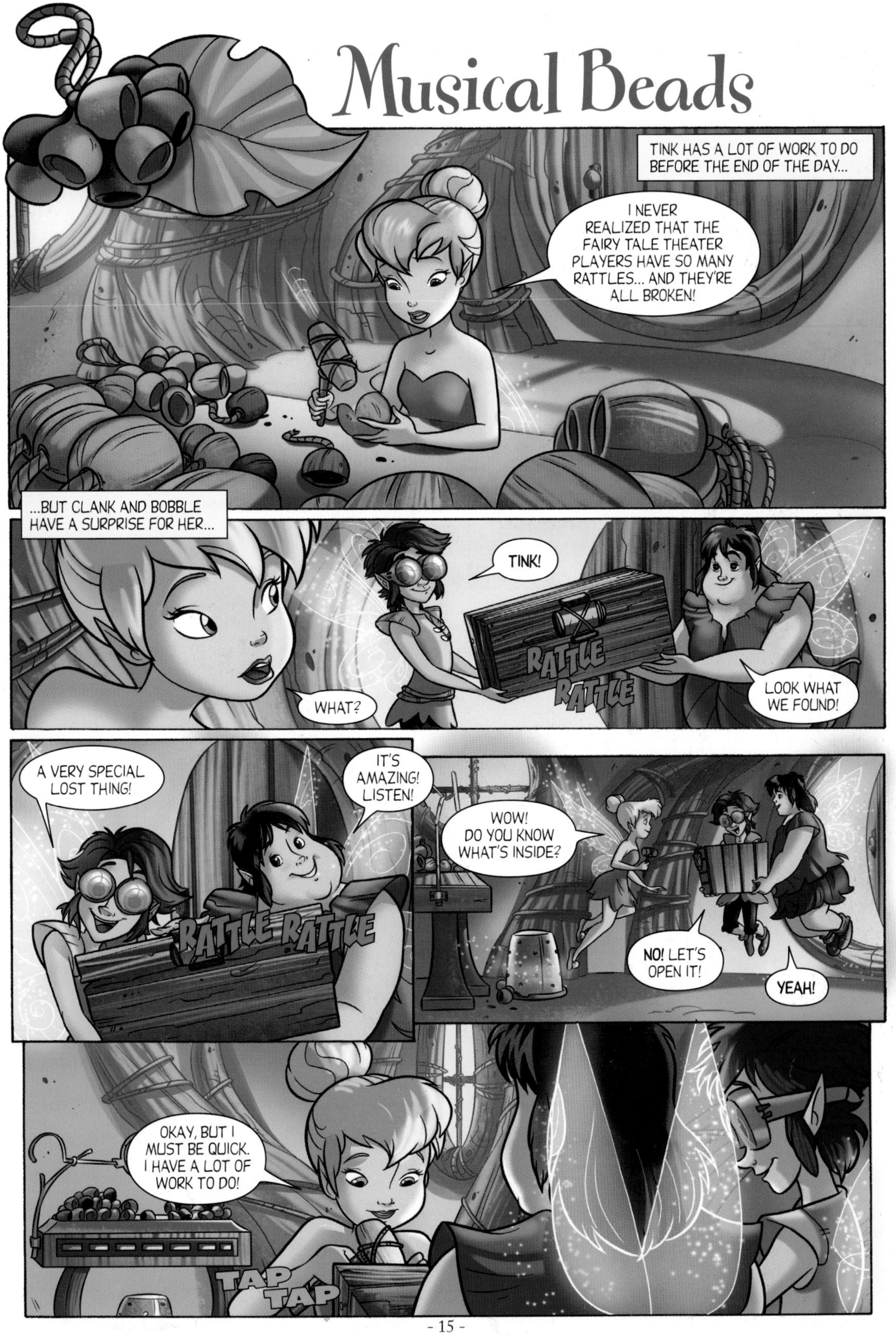
TINK HAS A LOT OF WORK TO DO BEFORE THE END OF THE DAY...
I NEVER REALIZED THAT THE FAIRY TALE THEATER PLAYERS HAVE SO MANY RATTLES... AND THEY'RE ALL BROKEN!
...BUT CLANK AND BOBBLE HAVE A SURPRISE FOR HER...
TINK!
WHAT?
RATTLE RATTLE
LOOK WHAT WE FOUND!
A VERY SPECIAL LOST THING!
IT'S AMAZING! LISTEN!
RATTLE RATTLE
WOW! DO YOU KNOW WHAT'S INSIDE?
NO! LET'S OPEN IT!
YEAH!
OKAY, BUT I MUST BE QUICK. I HAVE A LOT OF WORK TO DO!
TAP TAP

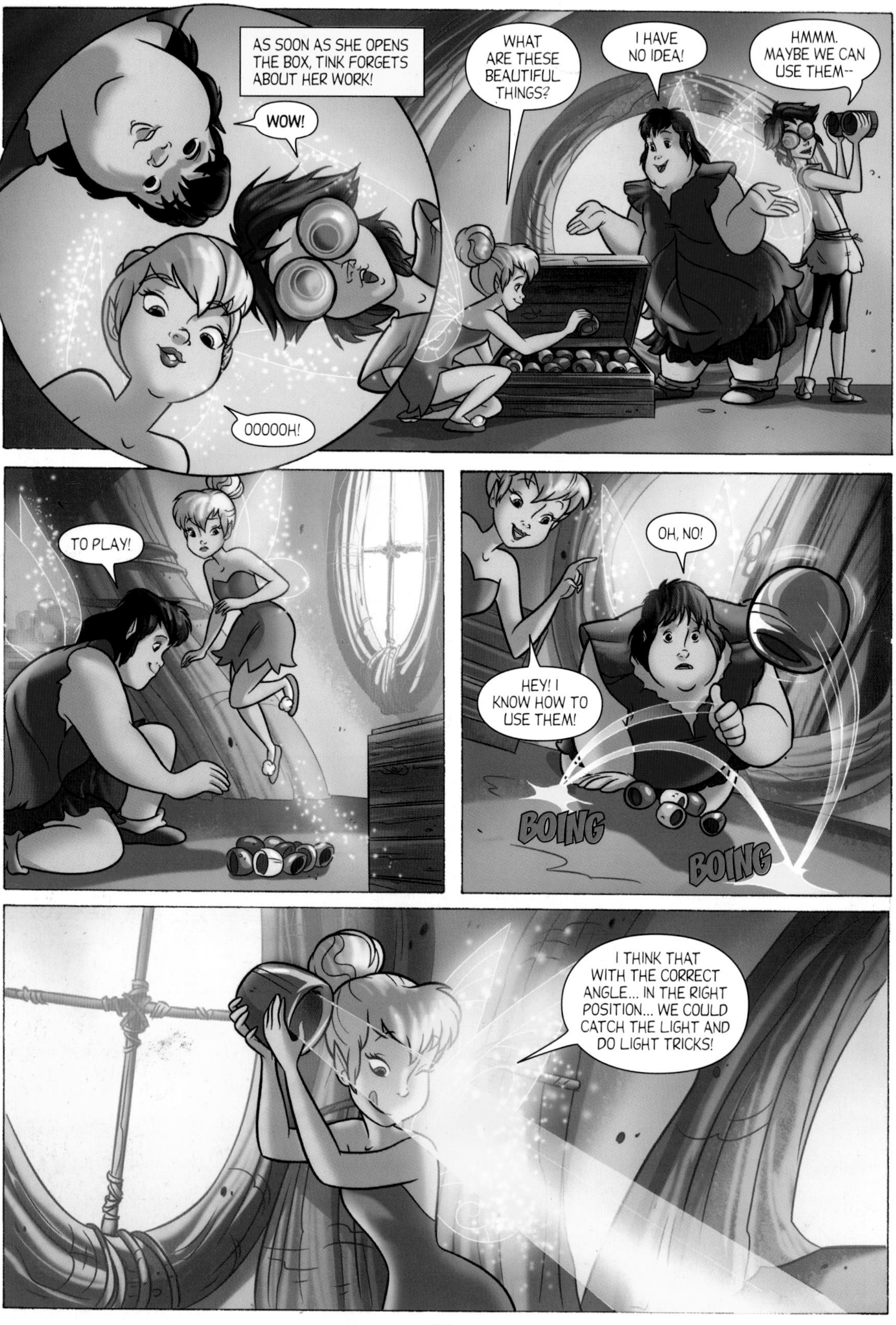
AS SOON AS SHE OPENS THE BOX, TINK FORGETS ABOUT HER WORK!
WOW!
OOOOOH!
WHAT ARE THESE BEAUTIFUL THINGS?
I HAVE NO IDEA!
HMMM. MAYBE WE CAN USE THEM--
TO PLAY!
HEY! I KNOW HOW TO USE THEM!
OH, NO!
BOING
BOING
I THINK THAT WITH THE CORRECT ANGLE... IN THE RIGHT POSITION... WE COULD CATCH THE LIGHT AND DO LIGHT TRICKS!

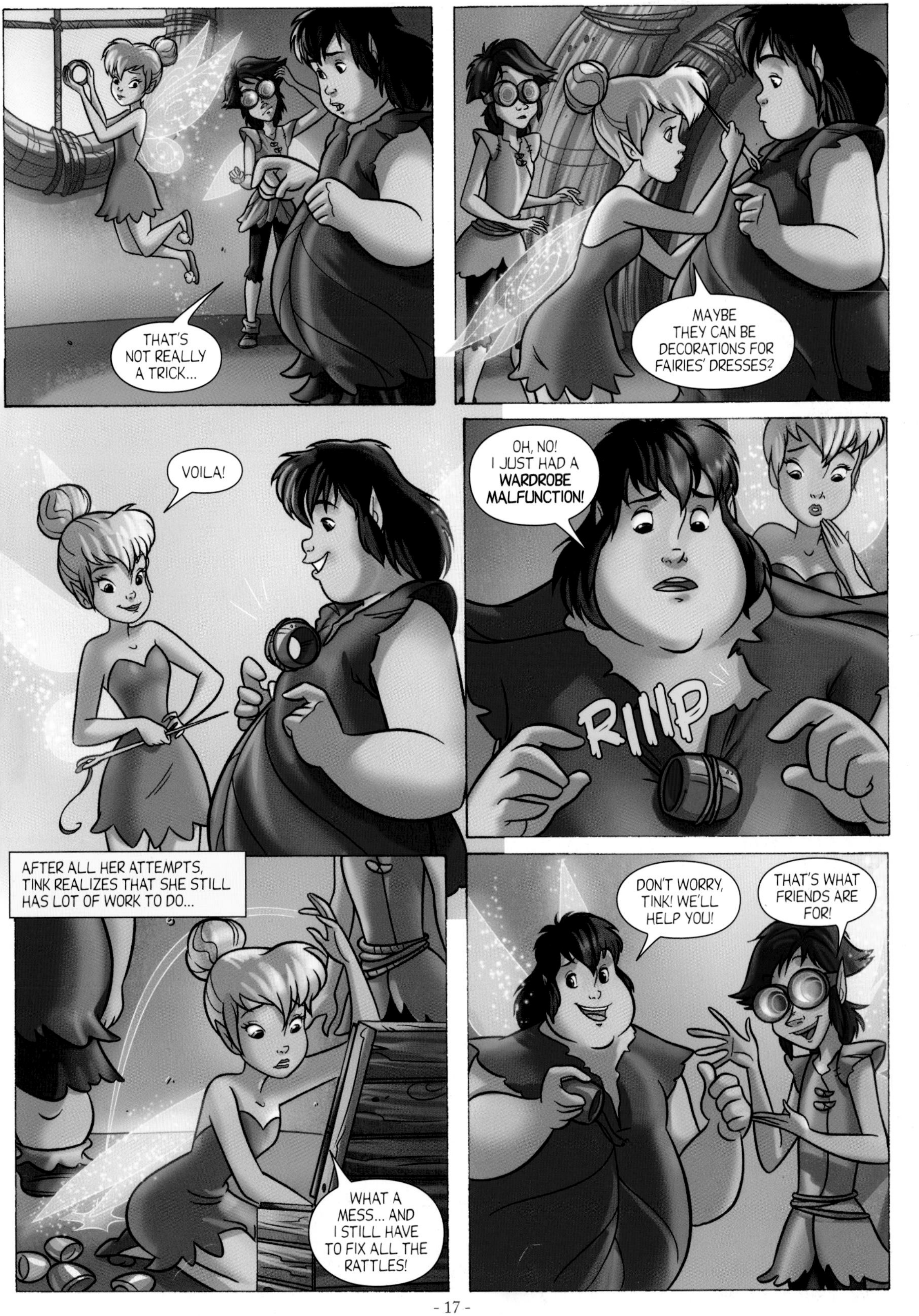
THAT'S NOT REALLY A TRICK...
MAYBE THEY CAN BE DECORATIONS FOR FAIRIES' DRESSES?
VOILA!
OH, NO! I JUST HAD A **WARDROBE MALFUNCTION!**
RIIIP
AFTER ALL HER ATTEMPTS, TINK REALIZES THAT SHE STILL HAS LOT OF WORK TO DO...
WHAT A MESS... AND I STILL HAVE TO FIX ALL THE RATTLES!
DON'T WORRY, TINK! WE'LL HELP YOU!
THAT'S WHAT FRIENDS ARE FOR!

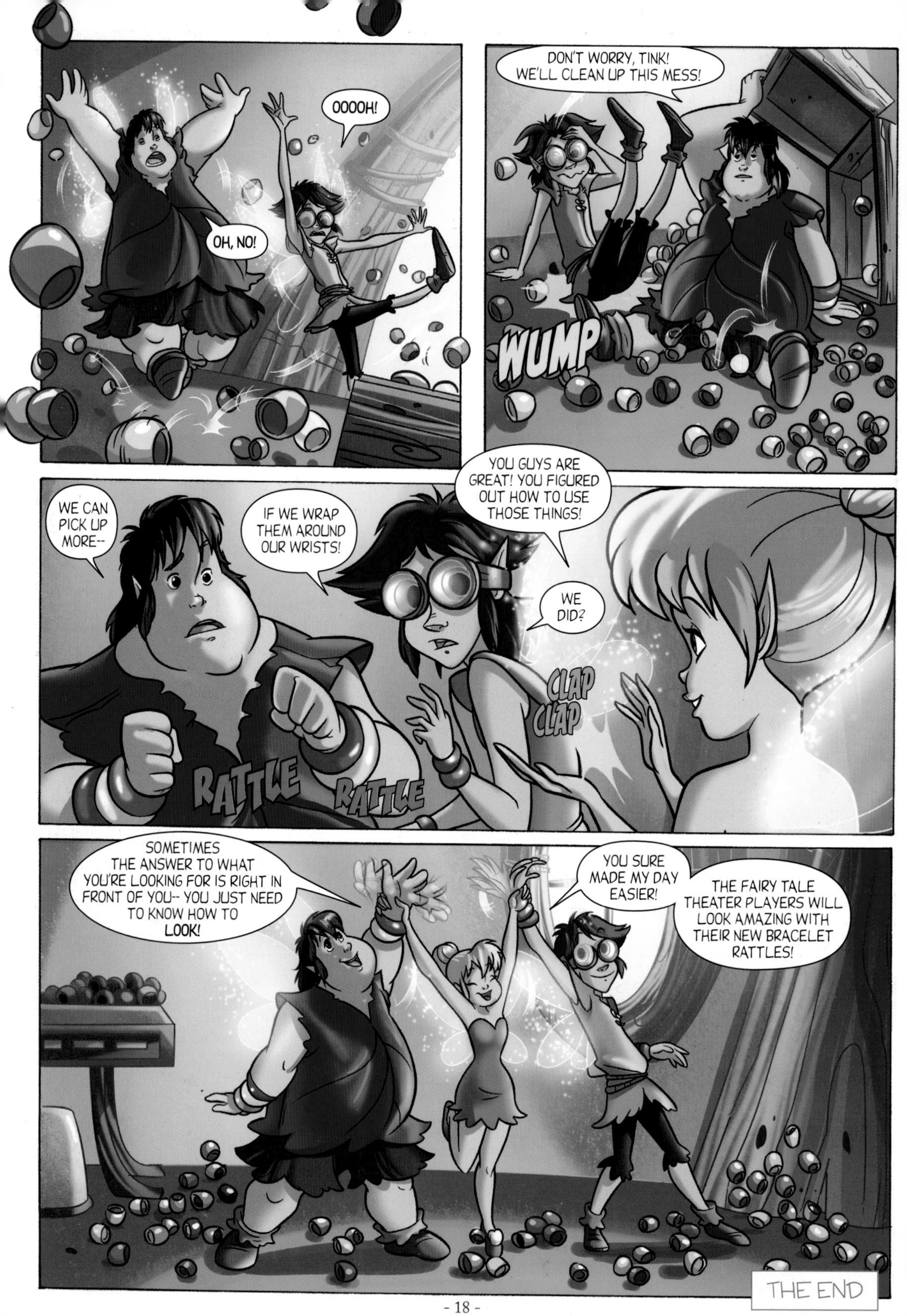

OOOOH!
OH, NO!
DON'T WORRY, TINK! WE'LL CLEAN UP THIS MESS!
WUMP
WE CAN PICK UP MORE--
IF WE WRAP THEM AROUND OUR WRISTS!
YOU GUYS ARE GREAT! YOU FIGURED OUT HOW TO USE THOSE THINGS!
WE DID?
CLAP CLAP
RATTLE RATTLE
SOMETIMES THE ANSWER TO WHAT YOU'RE LOOKING FOR IS RIGHT IN FRONT OF YOU-- YOU JUST NEED TO KNOW HOW TO **LOOK!**
YOU SURE MADE MY DAY EASIER!
THE FAIRY TALE THEATER PLAYERS WILL LOOK AMAZING WITH THEIR NEW BRACELET RATTLES!
THE END

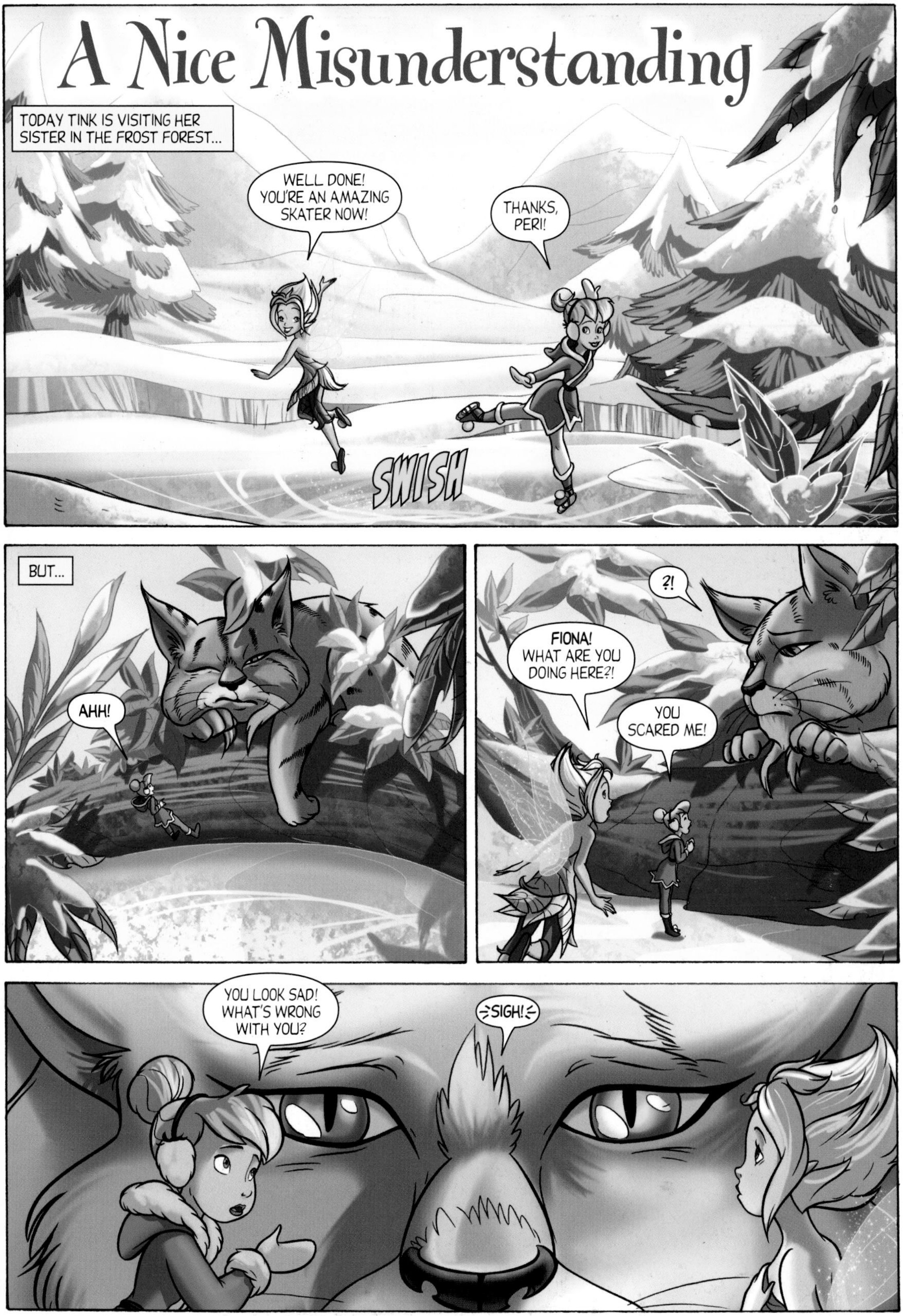
A Nice Misunderstanding
TODAY TINK IS VISITING HER SISTER IN THE FROST FOREST...
WELL DONE! YOU'RE AN AMAZING SKATER NOW!
THANKS, PERI!
SWISH
BUT...
AHH!
?!
FIONA! WHAT ARE YOU DOING HERE?!
YOU SCARED ME!
YOU LOOK SAD! WHAT'S WRONG WITH YOU?
SIGH!

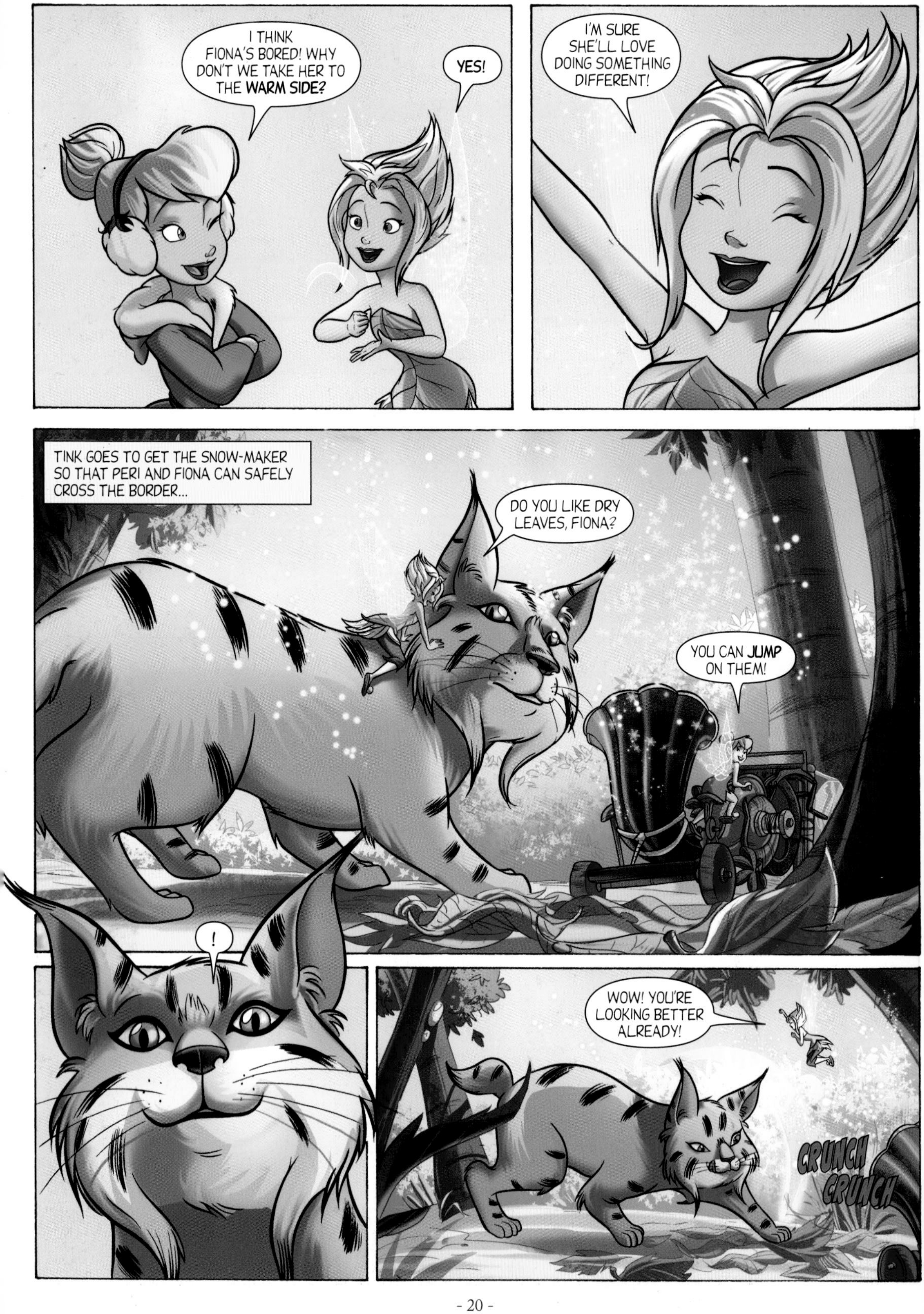
I THINK FIONA'S BORED! WHY DON'T WE TAKE HER TO THE **WARM SIDE?**
YES!
I'M SURE SHE'LL LOVE DOING SOMETHING DIFFERENT!
TINK GOES TO GET THE SNOW-MAKER SO THAT PERI AND FIONA CAN SAFELY CROSS THE BORDER...
DO YOU LIKE DRY LEAVES, FIONA?
YOU CAN **JUMP** ON THEM!
!
WOW! YOU'RE LOOKING BETTER ALREADY!
CRUNCH
CRUNCH

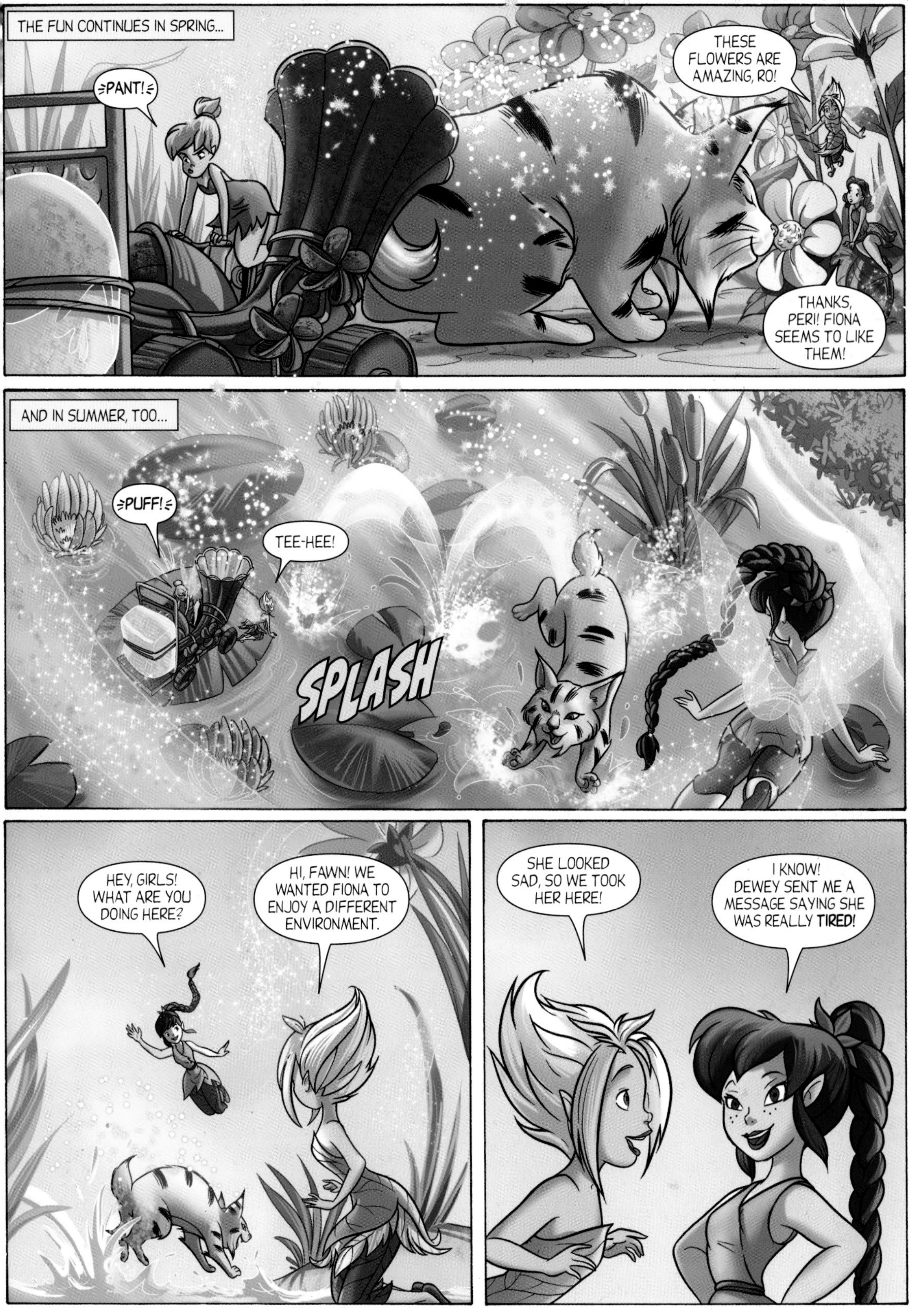
THE FUN CONTINUES IN SPRING...
PANT!
THESE FLOWERS ARE AMAZING, RO!
THANKS, PERI! FIONA SEEMS TO LIKE THEM!
AND IN SUMMER, TOO...
PUFF!
TEE-HEE!
SPLASH
HEY, GIRLS! WHAT ARE YOU DOING HERE?
HI, FAWN! WE WANTED FIONA TO ENJOY A DIFFERENT ENVIRONMENT.
SHE LOOKED SAD, SO WE TOOK HER HERE!
I KNOW! DEWEY SENT ME A MESSAGE SAYING SHE WAS REALLY TIRED!

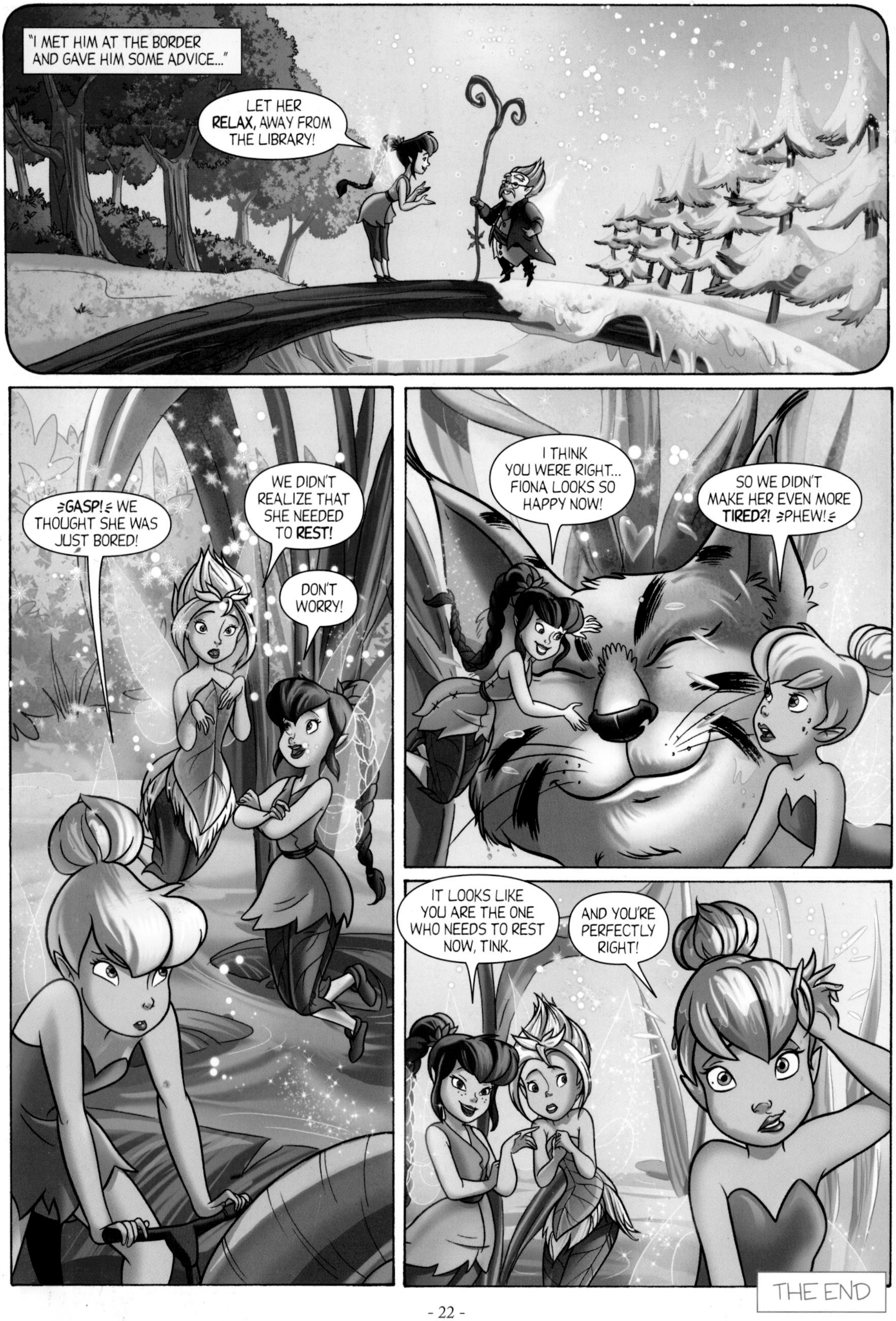
"I MET HIM AT THE BORDER AND GAVE HIM SOME ADVICE..."
LET HER RELAX, AWAY FROM THE LIBRARY!
GASP! WE THOUGHT SHE WAS JUST BORED!
WE DIDN'T REALIZE THAT SHE NEEDED TO REST!
DON'T WORRY!
I THINK YOU WERE RIGHT... FIONA LOOKS SO HAPPY NOW!
SO WE DIDN'T MAKE HER EVEN MORE TIRED?! PHEW!
IT LOOKS LIKE YOU ARE THE ONE WHO NEEDS TO REST NOW, TINK.
AND YOU'RE PERFECTLY RIGHT!
THE END

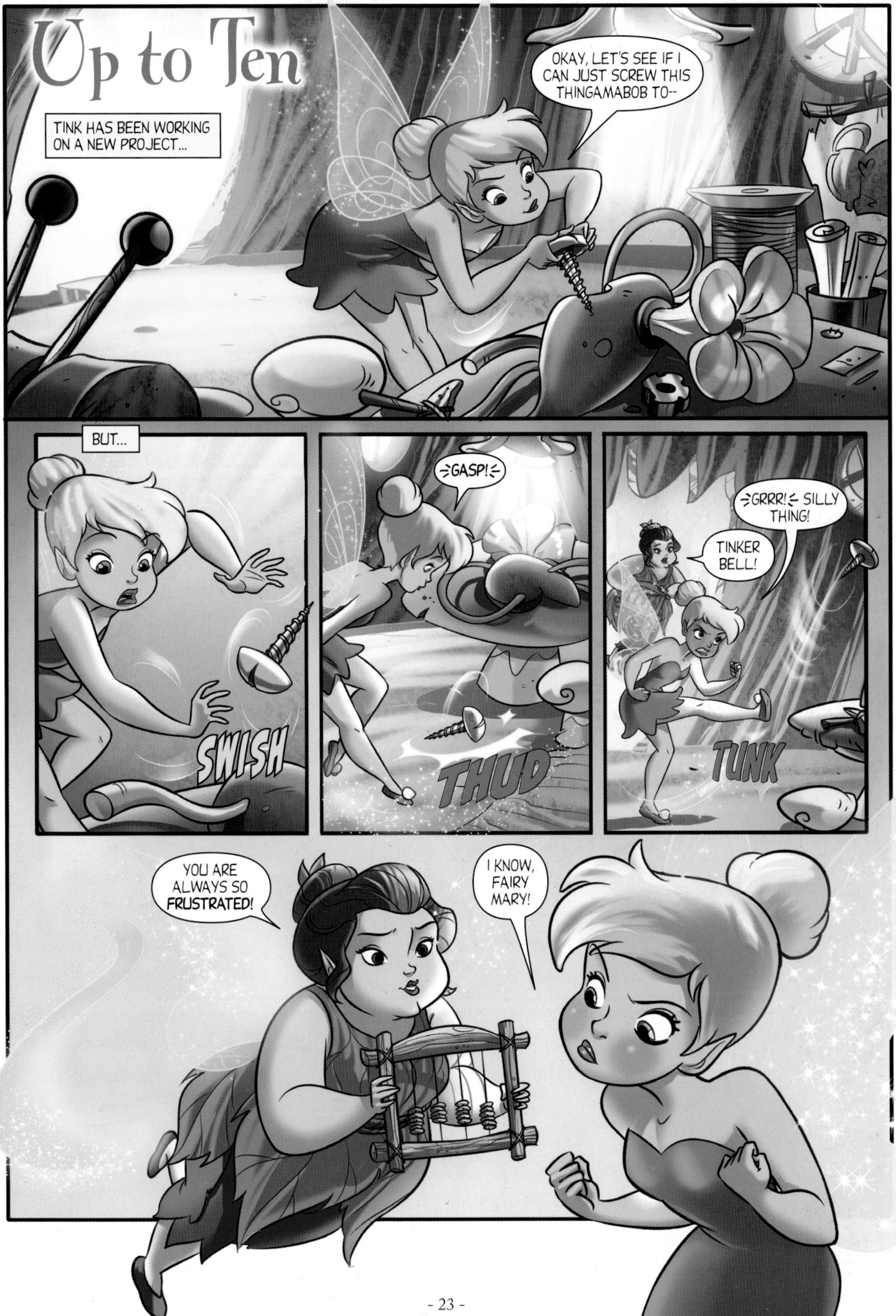

Up to Ten
TINK HAS BEEN WORKING ON A NEW PROJECT...
OKAY, LET'S SEE IF I CAN JUST SCREW THIS THINGAMABOB TO--
BUT...
SWISH
GASP!
THUD
GRRR! SILLY THING!
TINKER BELL!
TUNK
YOU ARE ALWAYS SO FRUSTRATED!
I KNOW, FAIRY MARY!

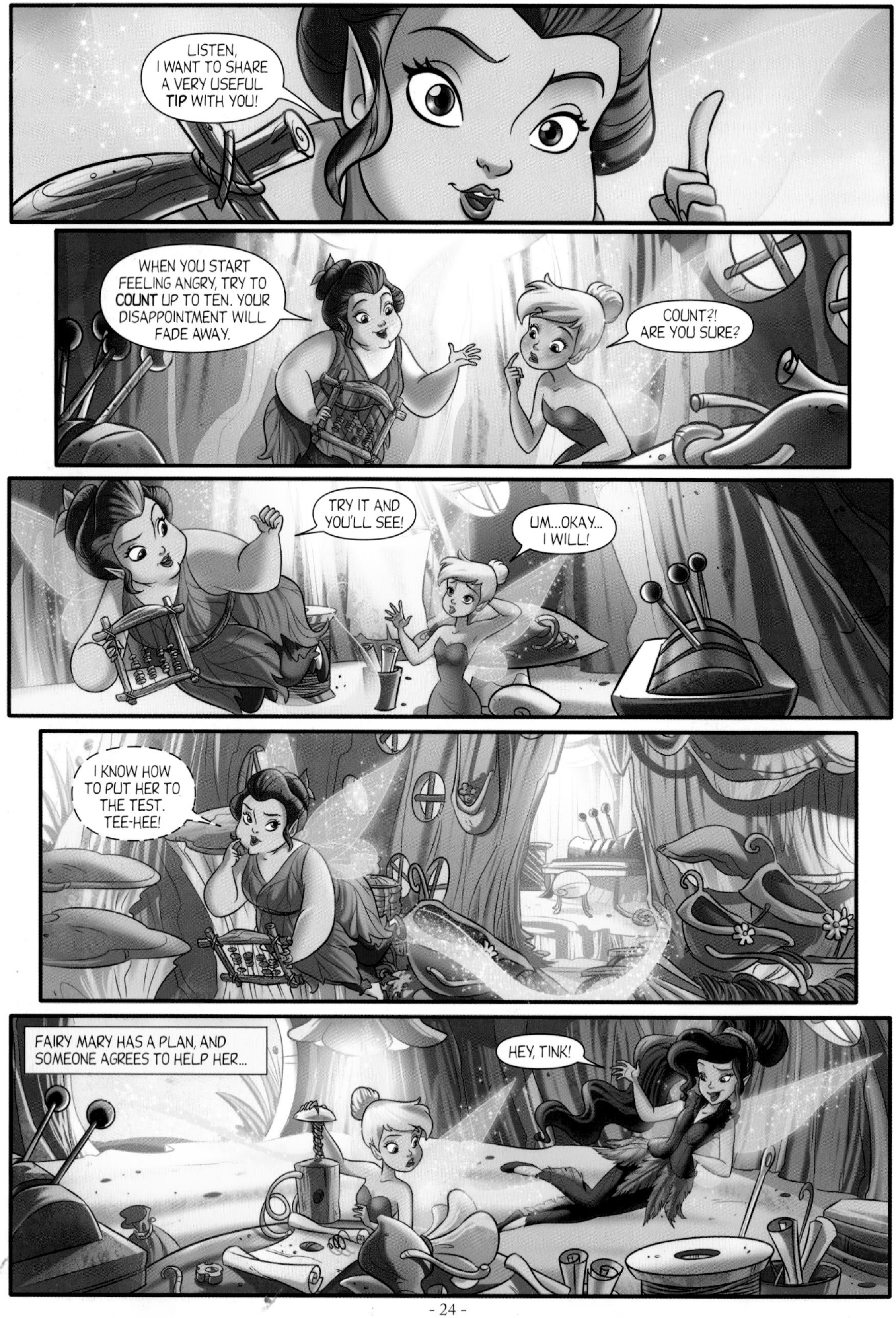
LISTEN, I WANT TO SHARE A VERY USEFUL **TIP** WITH YOU!
WHEN YOU START FEELING ANGRY, TRY TO **COUNT** UP TO TEN. YOUR DISAPPOINTMENT WILL FADE AWAY.
COUNT?! ARE YOU SURE?
TRY IT AND YOU'LL SEE!
UM...OKAY... I WILL!
I KNOW HOW TO PUT HER TO THE TEST. TEE-HEE!
FAIRY MARY HAS A PLAN, AND SOMEONE AGREES TO HELP HER...
HEY, TINK!

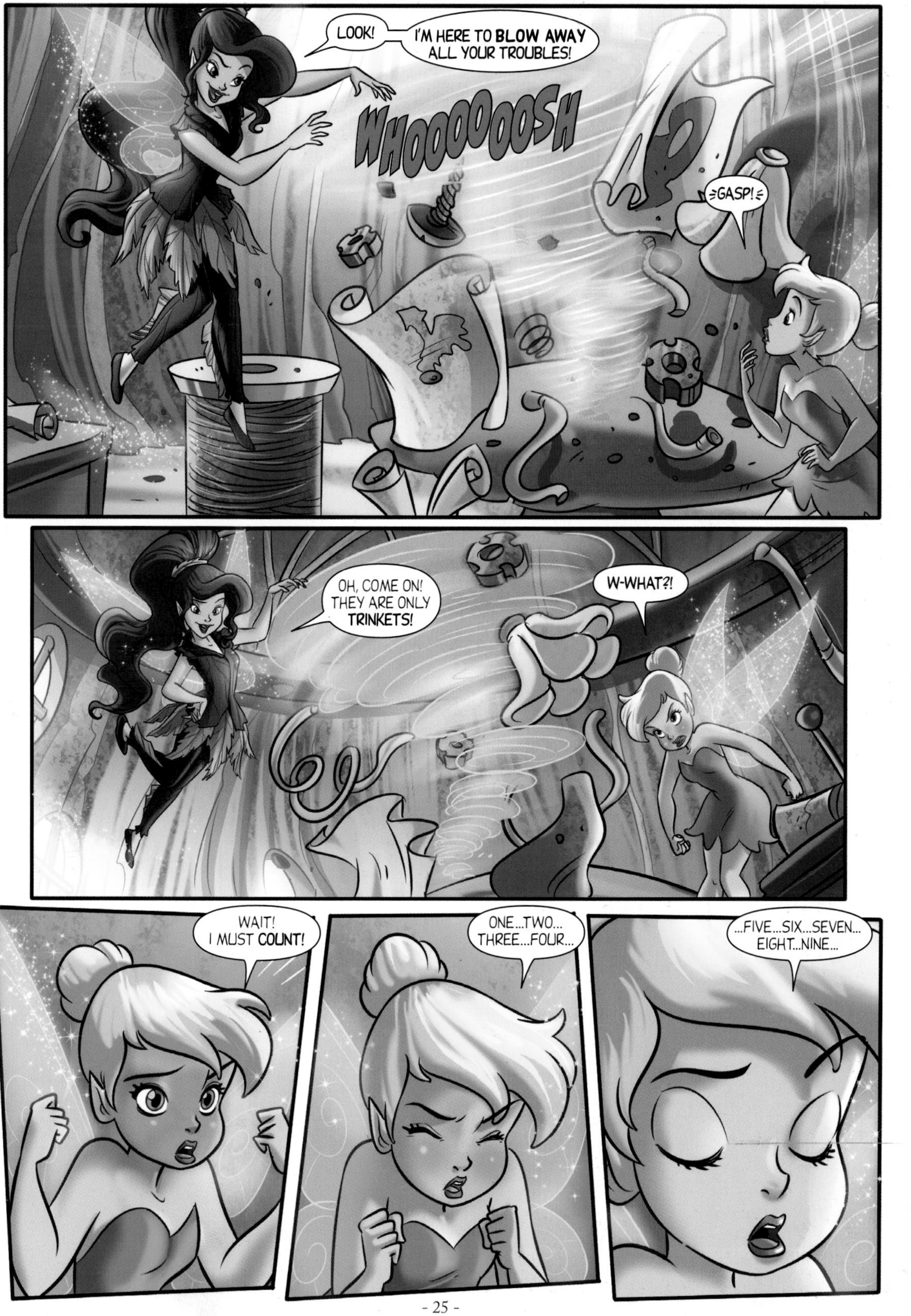
LOOK!
I'M HERE TO BLOW AWAY ALL YOUR TROUBLES!
WHOOOOOOOSH
GASP!
OH, COME ON! THEY ARE ONLY TRINKETS!
W-WHAT?!
WAIT! I MUST COUNT!
ONE...TWO... THREE...FOUR...
...FIVE...SIX...SEVEN... EIGHT...NINE...

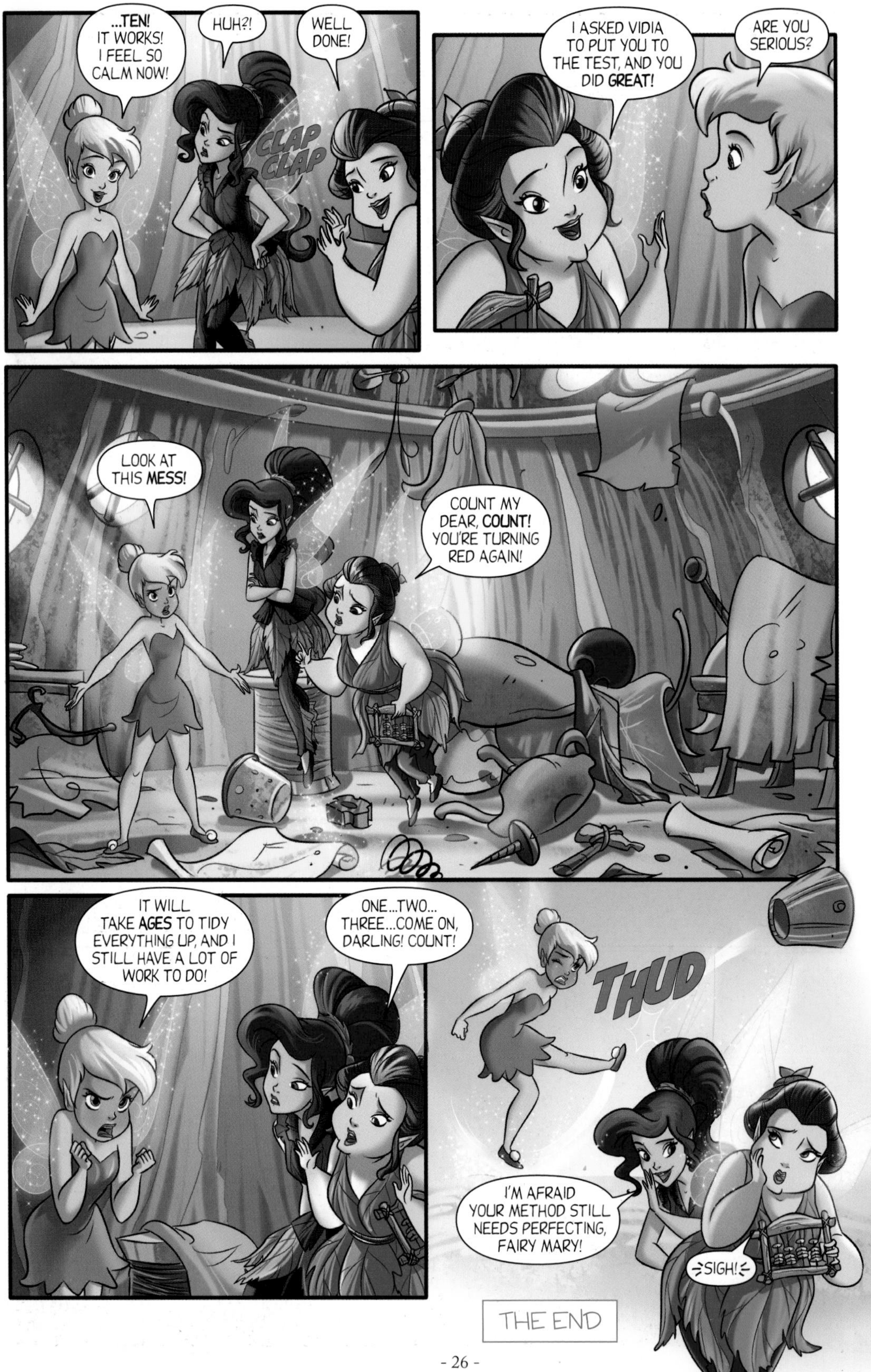
...TEN! IT WORKS! I FEEL SO CALM NOW!
HUH?!
WELL DONE!
CLAP CLAP
I ASKED VIDIA TO PUT YOU TO THE TEST, AND YOU DID GREAT!
ARE YOU SERIOUS?
LOOK AT THIS MESS!
COUNT MY DEAR, COUNT! YOU'RE TURNING RED AGAIN!
IT WILL TAKE AGES TO TIDY EVERYTHING UP, AND I STILL HAVE A LOT OF WORK TO DO!
ONE...TWO... THREE...COME ON, DARLING! COUNT!
THUD
I'M AFRAID YOUR METHOD STILL NEEDS PERFECTING, FAIRY MARY!
SIGH!
THE END

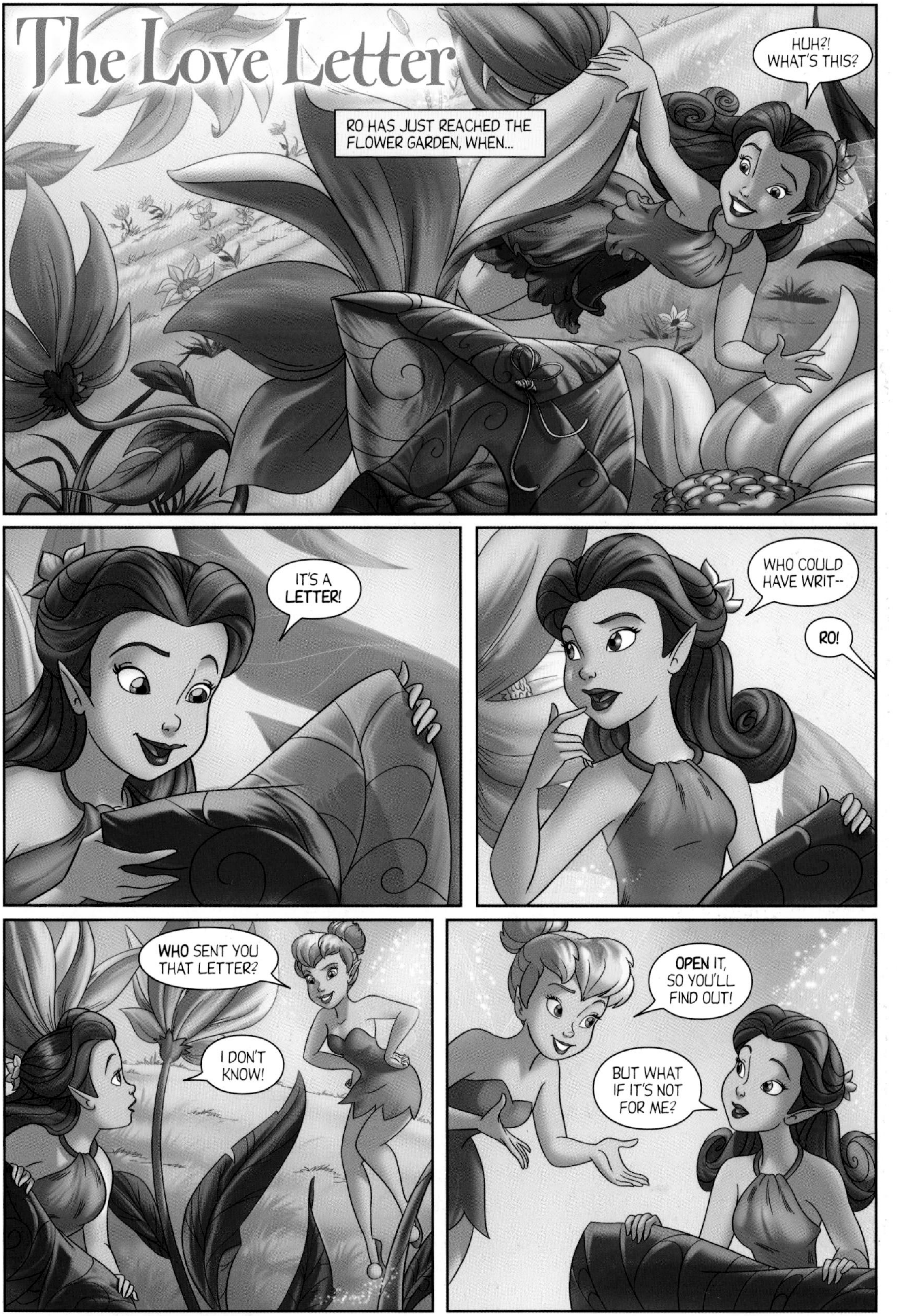
The Love Letter
RO HAS JUST REACHED THE FLOWER GARDEN, WHEN...
HUH?! WHAT'S THIS?
IT'S A **LETTER**!
WHO COULD HAVE WRIT--
RO!
WHO SENT YOU THAT LETTER?
I DON'T KNOW!
OPEN IT, SO YOU'LL FIND OUT!
BUT WHAT IF IT'S NOT FOR ME?

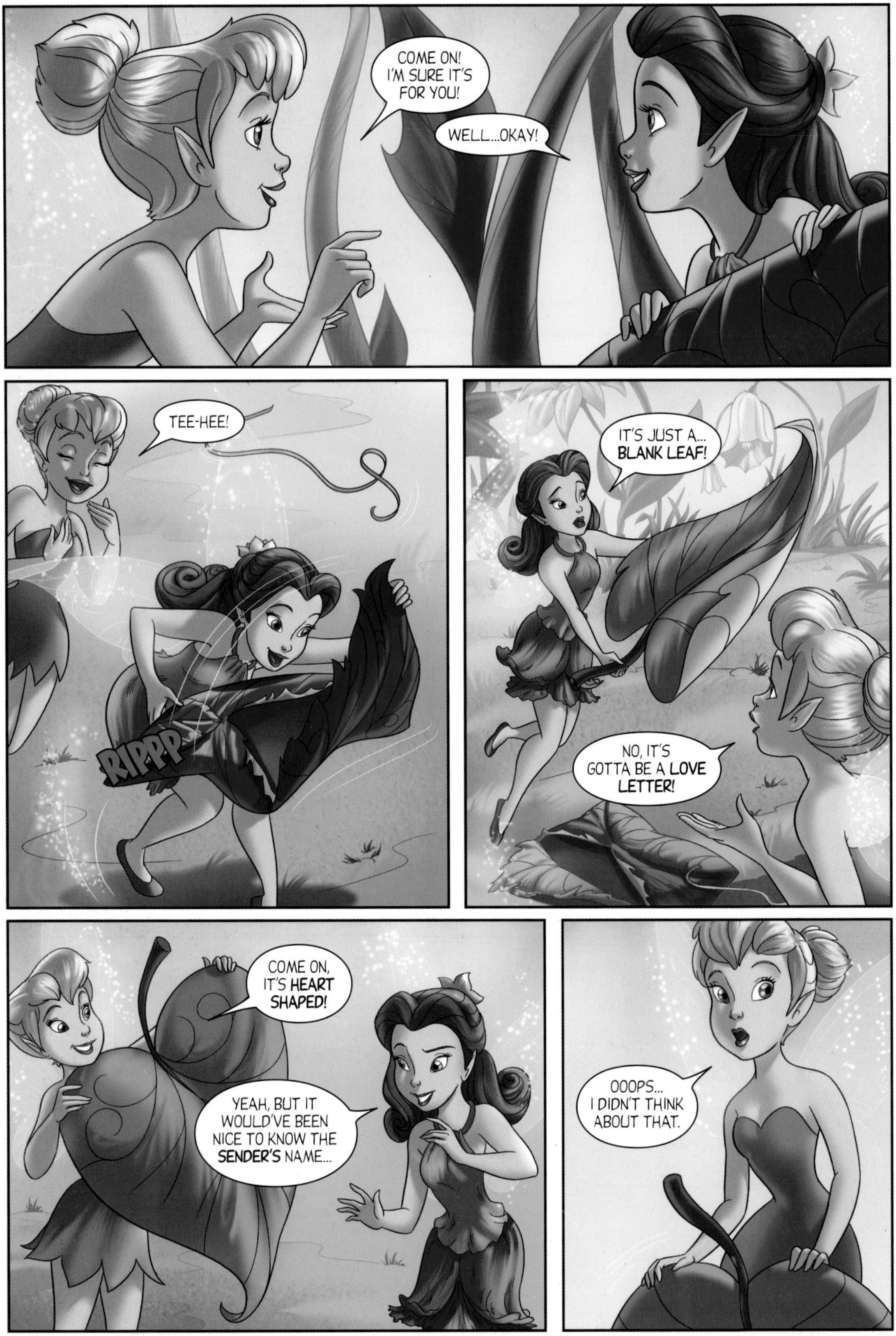
COME ON! I'M SURE IT'S FOR YOU!
WELL...OKAY!
TEE-HEE!
RIPPP
IT'S JUST A... **BLANK LEAF!**
NO, IT'S GOTTA BE A **LOVE LETTER!**
COME ON, IT'S **HEART SHAPED!**
YEAH, BUT IT WOULD'VE BEEN NICE TO KNOW THE **SENDER'S** NAME...
OOOPS... I DIDN'T THINK ABOUT THAT.

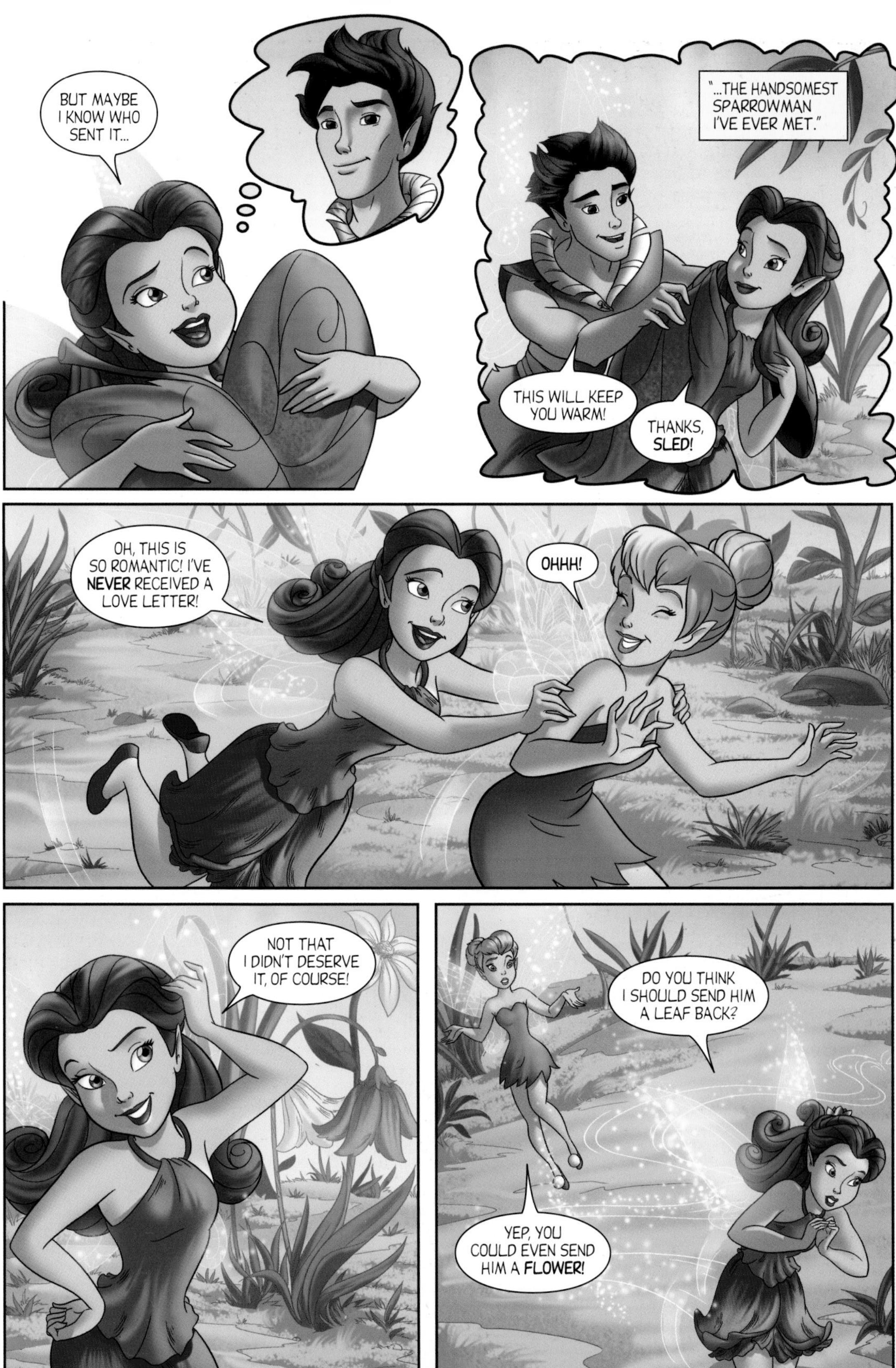
BUT MAYBE I KNOW WHO SENT IT...
"...THE HANDSOMEST SPARROWMAN I'VE EVER MET."
THIS WILL KEEP YOU WARM!
THANKS, **SLED!**
OH, THIS IS SO ROMANTIC! I'VE **NEVER** RECEIVED A LOVE LETTER!
OHHH!
NOT THAT I DIDN'T DESERVE IT, OF COURSE!
DO YOU THINK I SHOULD SEND HIM A LEAF BACK?
YEP, YOU COULD EVEN SEND HIM A **FLOWER!**

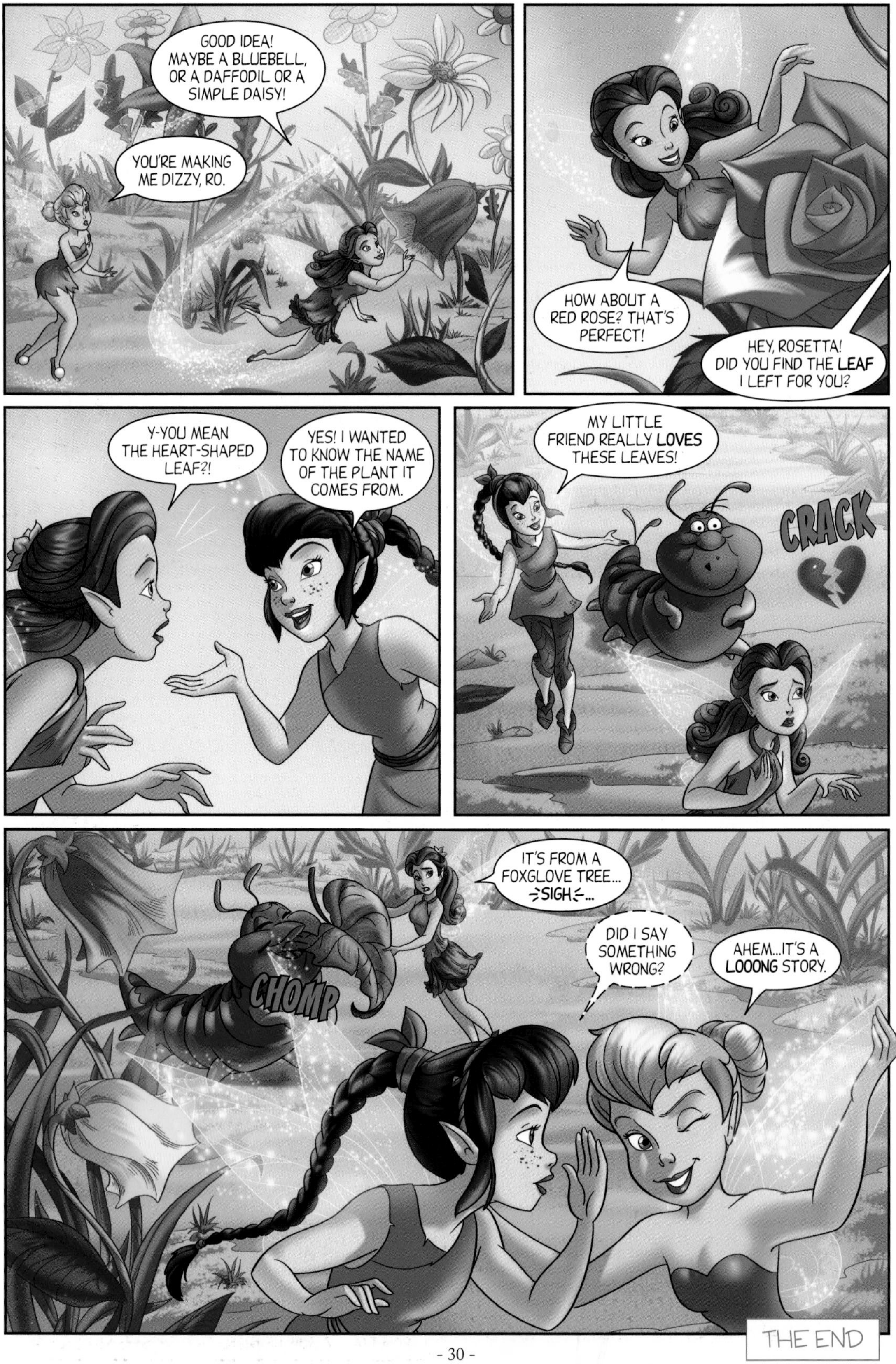
GOOD IDEA! MAYBE A BLUEBELL, OR A DAFFODIL OR A SIMPLE DAISY!
YOU'RE MAKING ME DIZZY, RO.
HOW ABOUT A RED ROSE? THAT'S PERFECT!
HEY, ROSETTA! DID YOU FIND THE **LEAF** I LEFT FOR YOU?
Y-YOU MEAN THE HEART-SHAPED LEAF?!
YES! I WANTED TO KNOW THE NAME OF THE PLANT IT COMES FROM.
MY LITTLE FRIEND REALLY **LOVES** THESE LEAVES!
CRACK
IT'S FROM A FOXGLOVE TREE... **SIGH**...
CHOMP
DID I SAY SOMETHING WRONG?
AHEM...IT'S A **LOOONG** STORY.
THE END

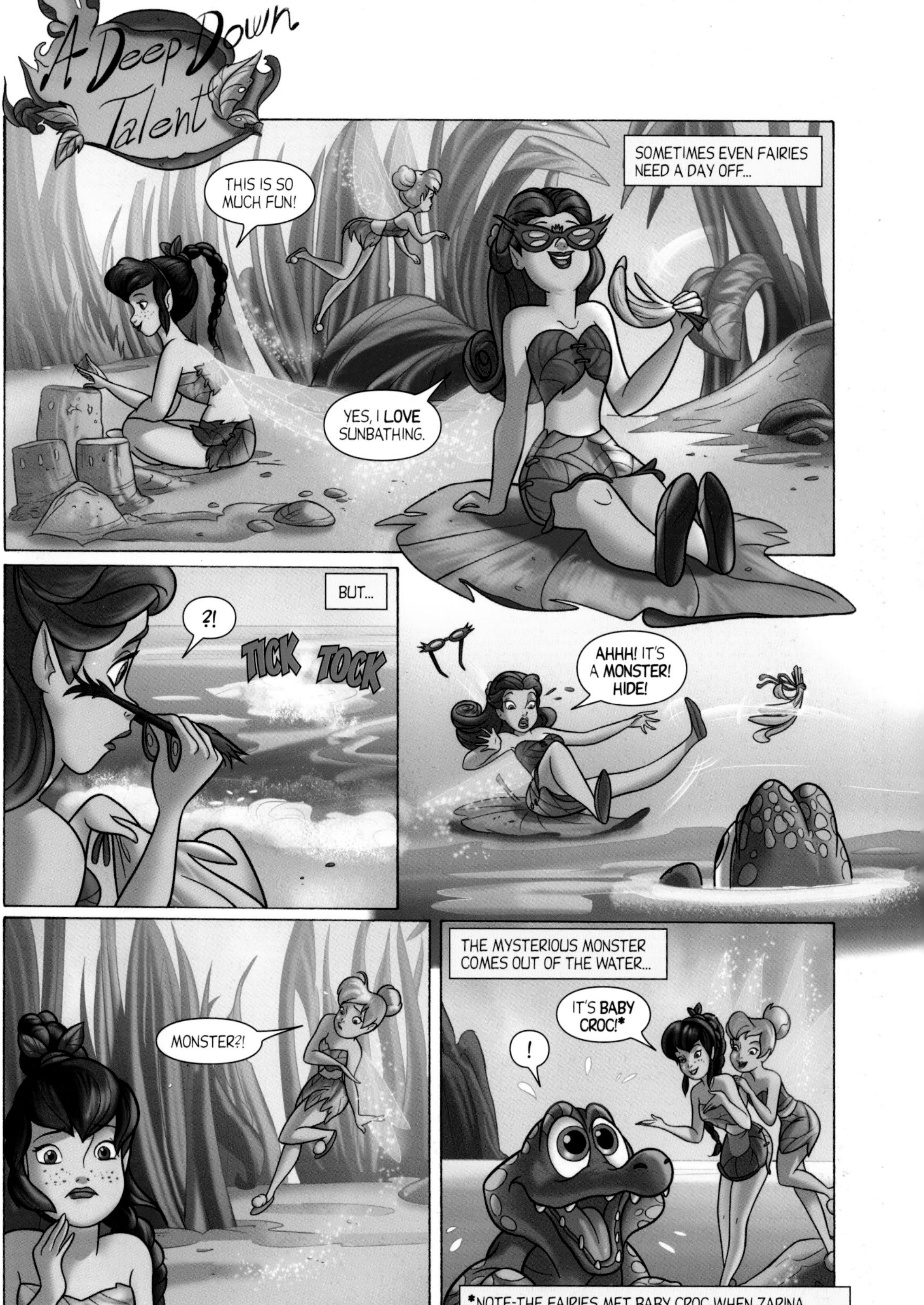
A Deep-Down Talent
SOMETIMES EVEN FAIRIES NEED A DAY OFF...
THIS IS SO MUCH FUN!
YES, I LOVE SUNBATHING.
BUT...
?!
TICK TOCK
AHHH! IT'S A MONSTER! HIDE!
MONSTER?!
THE MYSTERIOUS MONSTER COMES OUT OF THE WATER...
!
IT'S BABY CROC!*
*NOTE-THE FAIRIES MET BABY CROC WHEN ZARINA SWITCHED THEIR TALENTS. HE IMPRINTED ON ROSETTA, AND NOW HE THINKS THAT SHE'S HIS MOTHER.

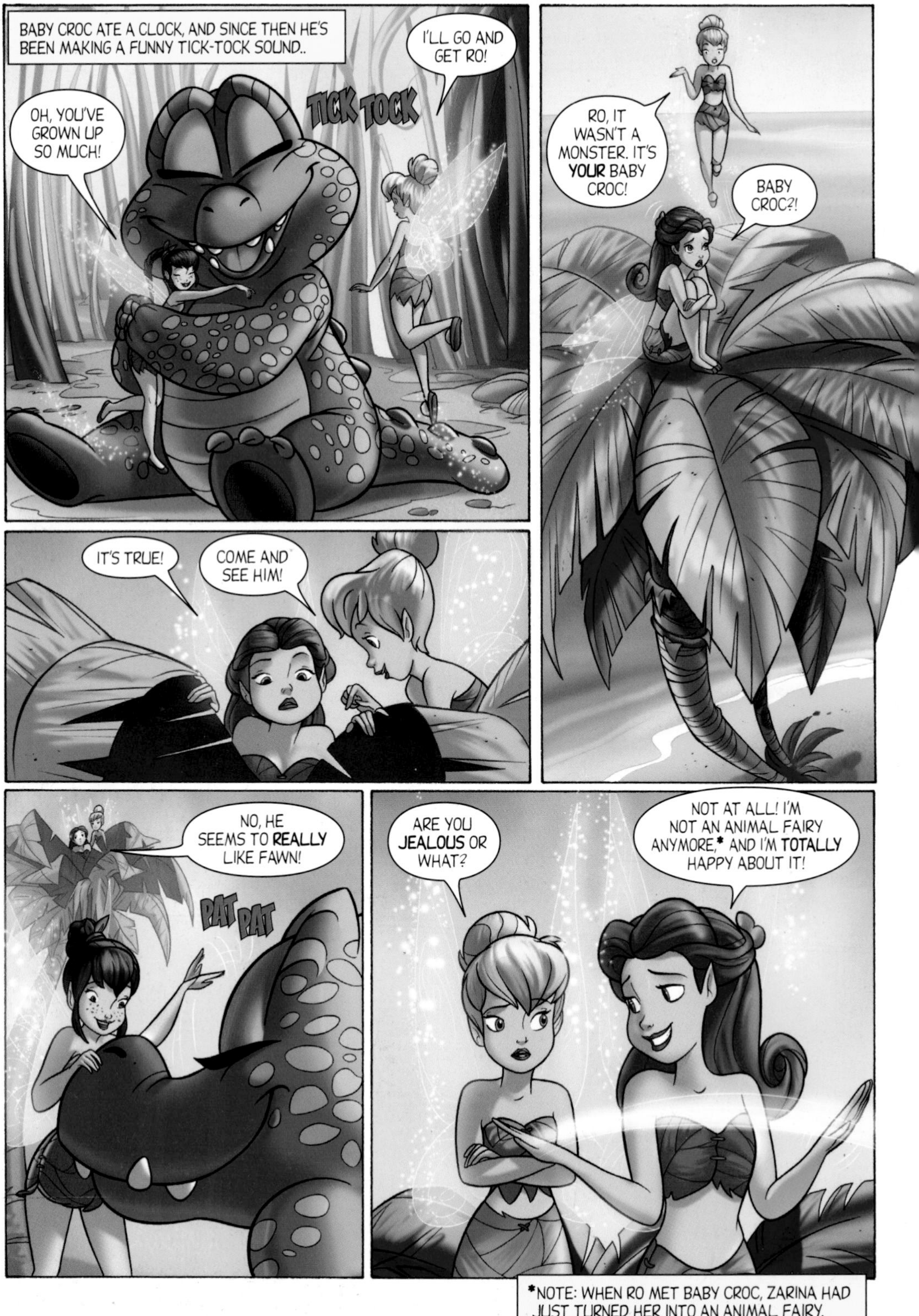
BABY CROC ATE A CLOCK, AND SINCE THEN HE'S BEEN MAKING A FUNNY TICK-TOCK SOUND..
OH, YOU'VE GROWN UP SO MUCH!
I'LL GO AND GET RO!
TICK TOCK
RO, IT WASN'T A MONSTER. IT'S YOUR BABY CROC!
BABY CROC?!
IT'S TRUE!
COME AND SEE HIM!
NO, HE SEEMS TO REALLY LIKE FAWN!
PAT PAT
ARE YOU JEALOUS OR WHAT?
NOT AT ALL! I'M NOT AN ANIMAL FAIRY ANYMORE,* AND I'M TOTALLY HAPPY ABOUT IT!
*NOTE: WHEN RO MET BABY CROC, ZARINA HAD JUST TURNED HER INTO AN ANIMAL FAIRY.

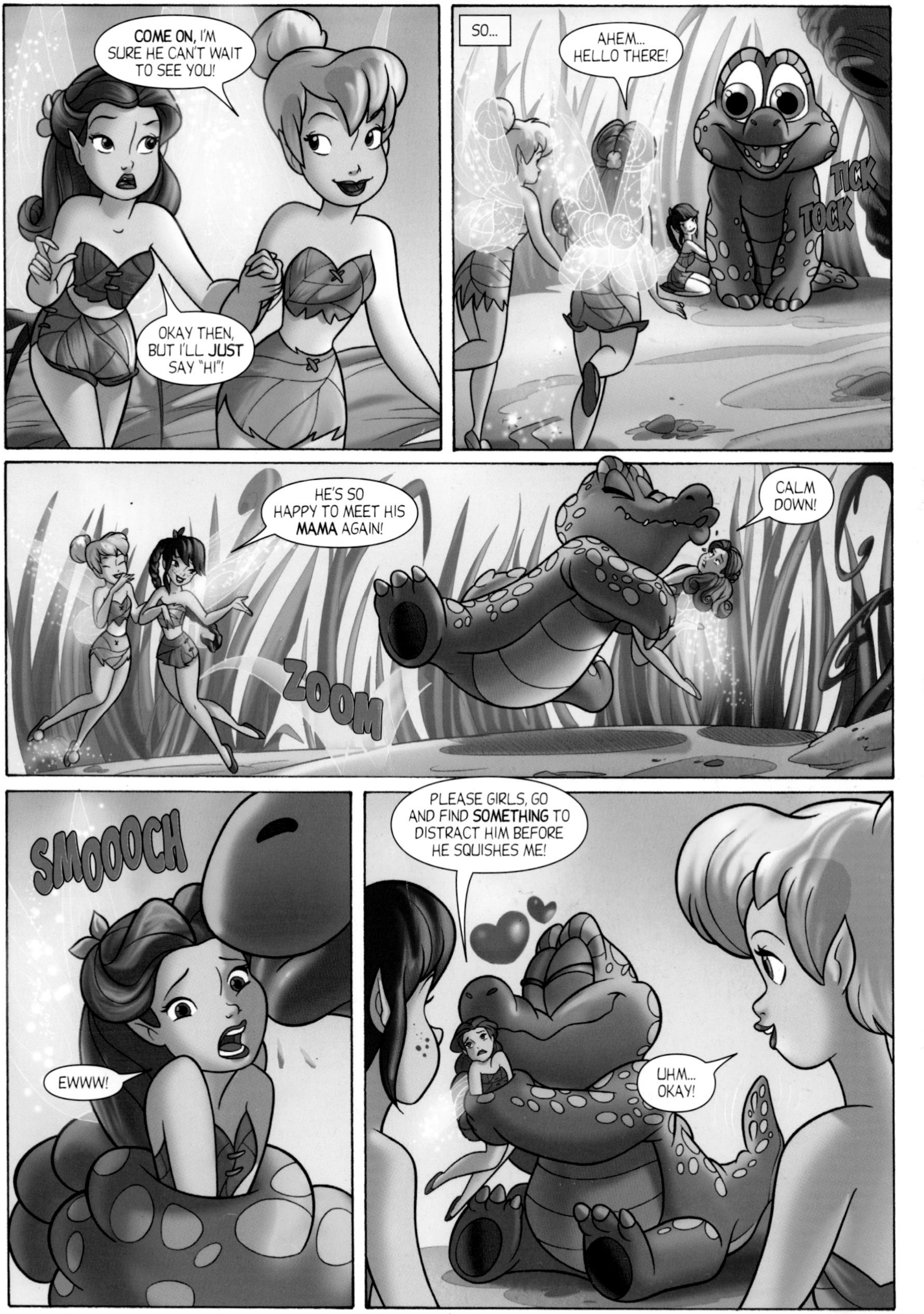
COME ON, I'M SURE HE CAN'T WAIT TO SEE YOU!
OKAY THEN, BUT I'LL JUST SAY "HI"!
SO...
AHEM... HELLO THERE!
TICK
TOCK
HE'S SO HAPPY TO MEET HIS MAMA AGAIN!
CALM DOWN!
ZOOM
SMOOOCH
EWWW!
PLEASE GIRLS, GO AND FIND SOMETHING TO DISTRACT HIM BEFORE HE SQUISHES ME!
UHM... OKAY!

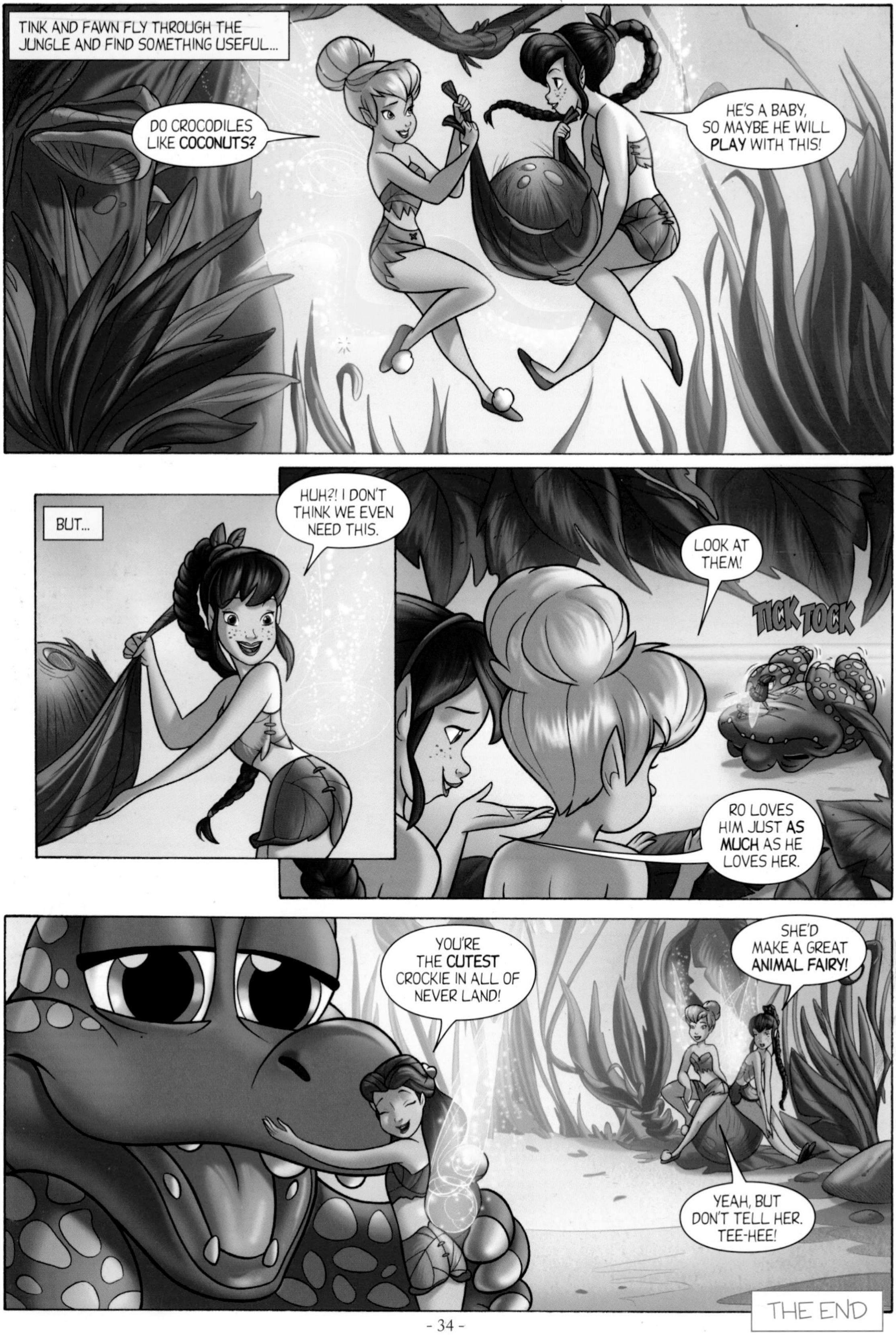
TINK AND FAWN FLY THROUGH THE JUNGLE AND FIND SOMETHING USEFUL...
DO CROCODILES LIKE COCONUTS?
HE'S A BABY, SO MAYBE HE WILL PLAY WITH THIS!
BUT...
HUH?! I DON'T THINK WE EVEN NEED THIS.
LOOK AT THEM!
TICK TOCK
RO LOVES HIM JUST AS MUCH AS HE LOVES HER.
YOU'RE THE CUTEST CROCKIE IN ALL OF NEVER LAND!
SHE'D MAKE A GREAT ANIMAL FAIRY!
YEAH, BUT DON'T TELL HER. TEE-HEE!
THE END

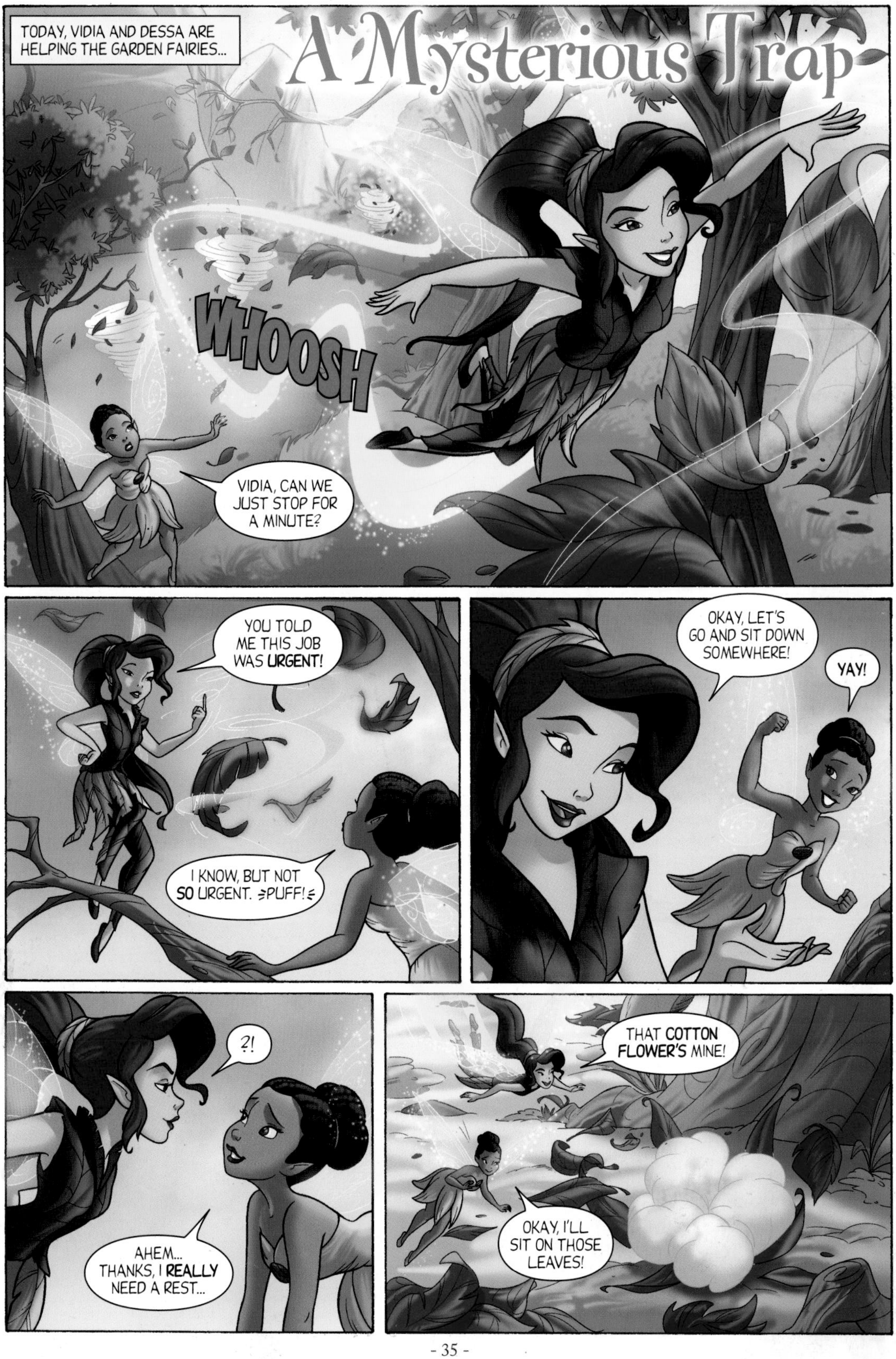
TODAY, VIDIA AND DESSA ARE HELPING THE GARDEN FAIRIES...
A Mysterious Trap
WHOOSH
VIDIA, CAN WE JUST STOP FOR A MINUTE?
YOU TOLD ME THIS JOB WAS URGENT!
I KNOW, BUT NOT SO URGENT. PUFF!
OKAY, LET'S GO AND SIT DOWN SOMEWHERE!
YAY!
?!
AHEM... THANKS, I REALLY NEED A REST...
THAT COTTON FLOWER'S MINE!
OKAY, I'LL SIT ON THOSE LEAVES!

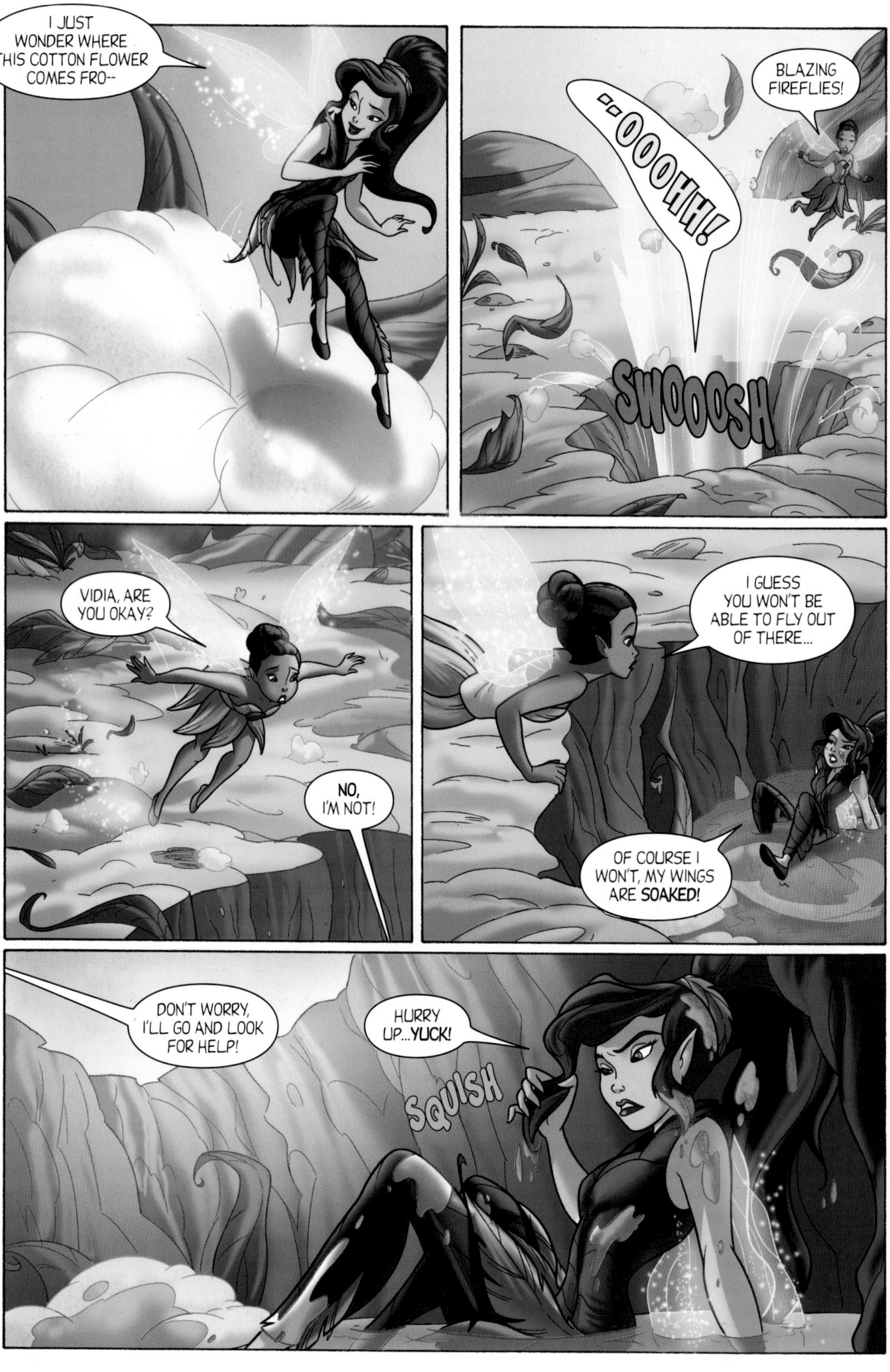
I JUST WONDER WHERE THIS COTTON FLOWER COMES FRO--
BLAZING FIREFLIES!
--OOOHH!
SWOOOSH
VIDIA, ARE YOU OKAY?
NO, I'M NOT!
I GUESS YOU WON'T BE ABLE TO FLY OUT OF THERE...
OF COURSE I WON'T, MY WINGS ARE **SOAKED!**
DON'T WORRY, I'LL GO AND LOOK FOR HELP!
HURRY UP...**YUCK!**
SQUISH

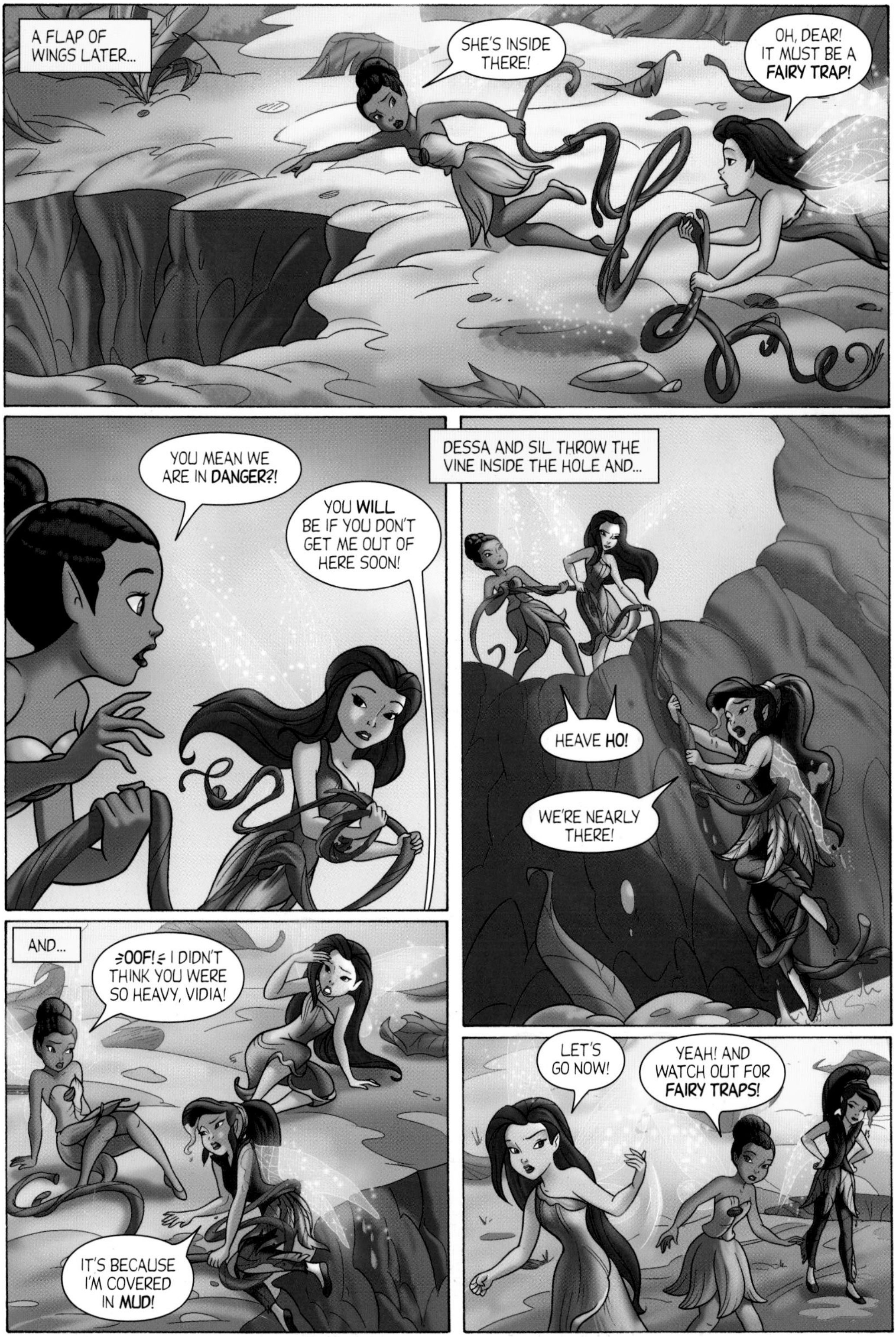
A FLAP OF WINGS LATER...
SHE'S INSIDE THERE!
OH, DEAR! IT MUST BE A **FAIRY TRAP!**
YOU MEAN WE ARE IN **DANGER?!**
YOU **WILL** BE IF YOU DON'T GET ME OUT OF HERE SOON!
DESSA AND SIL THROW THE VINE INSIDE THE HOLE AND...
HEAVE **HO!**
WE'RE NEARLY THERE!
AND...
OOF! I DIDN'T THINK YOU WERE SO HEAVY, VIDIA!
IT'S BECAUSE I'M COVERED IN **MUD!**
LET'S GO NOW!
YEAH! AND WATCH OUT FOR **FAIRY TRAPS!**

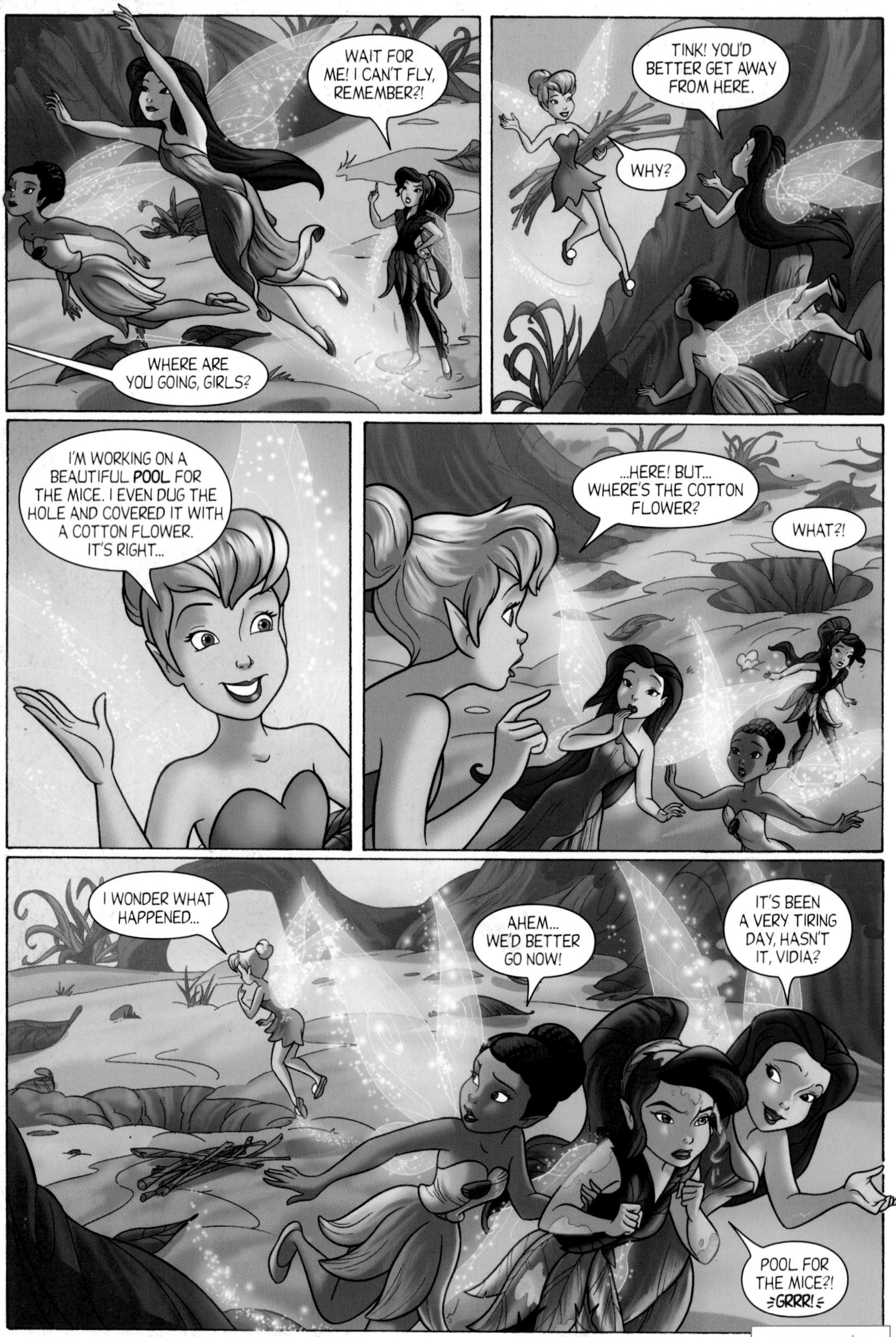
WAIT FOR ME! I CAN'T FLY, REMEMBER?!
WHERE ARE YOU GOING, GIRLS?
TINK! YOU'D BETTER GET AWAY FROM HERE.
WHY?
I'M WORKING ON A BEAUTIFUL **POOL** FOR THE MICE. I EVEN DUG THE HOLE AND COVERED IT WITH A COTTON FLOWER. IT'S RIGHT...
...HERE! BUT... WHERE'S THE COTTON FLOWER?
WHAT?!
I WONDER WHAT HAPPENED...
AHEM... WE'D BETTER GO NOW!
IT'S BEEN A VERY TIRING DAY, HASN'T IT, VIDIA?
POOL FOR THE MICE?! GRRR!
THE END

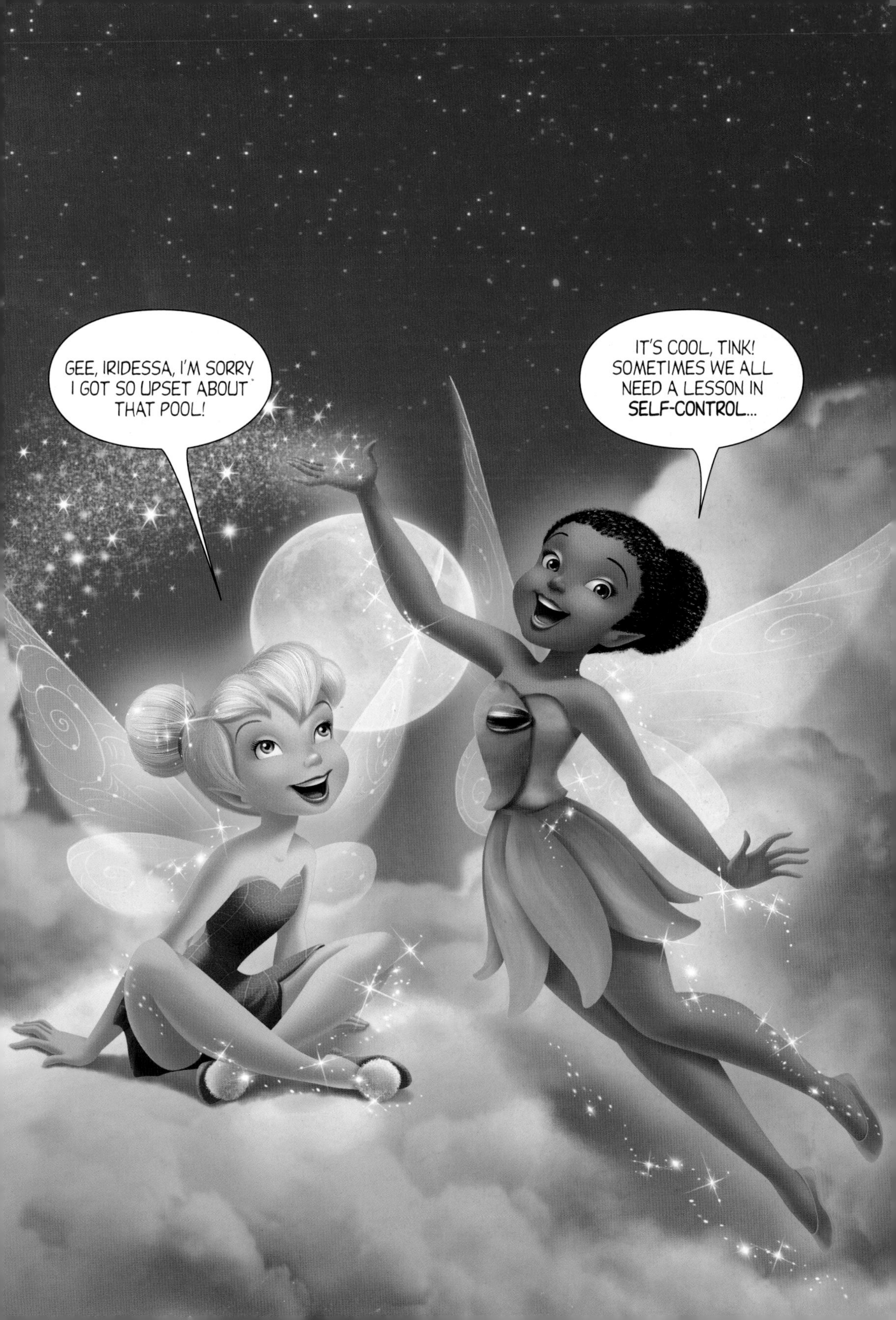
GEE, IRIDESSA, I'M SORRY I GOT SO UPSET ABOUT THAT POOL!
IT'S COOL, TINK! SOMETIMES WE ALL NEED A LESSON IN SELF-CONTROL...

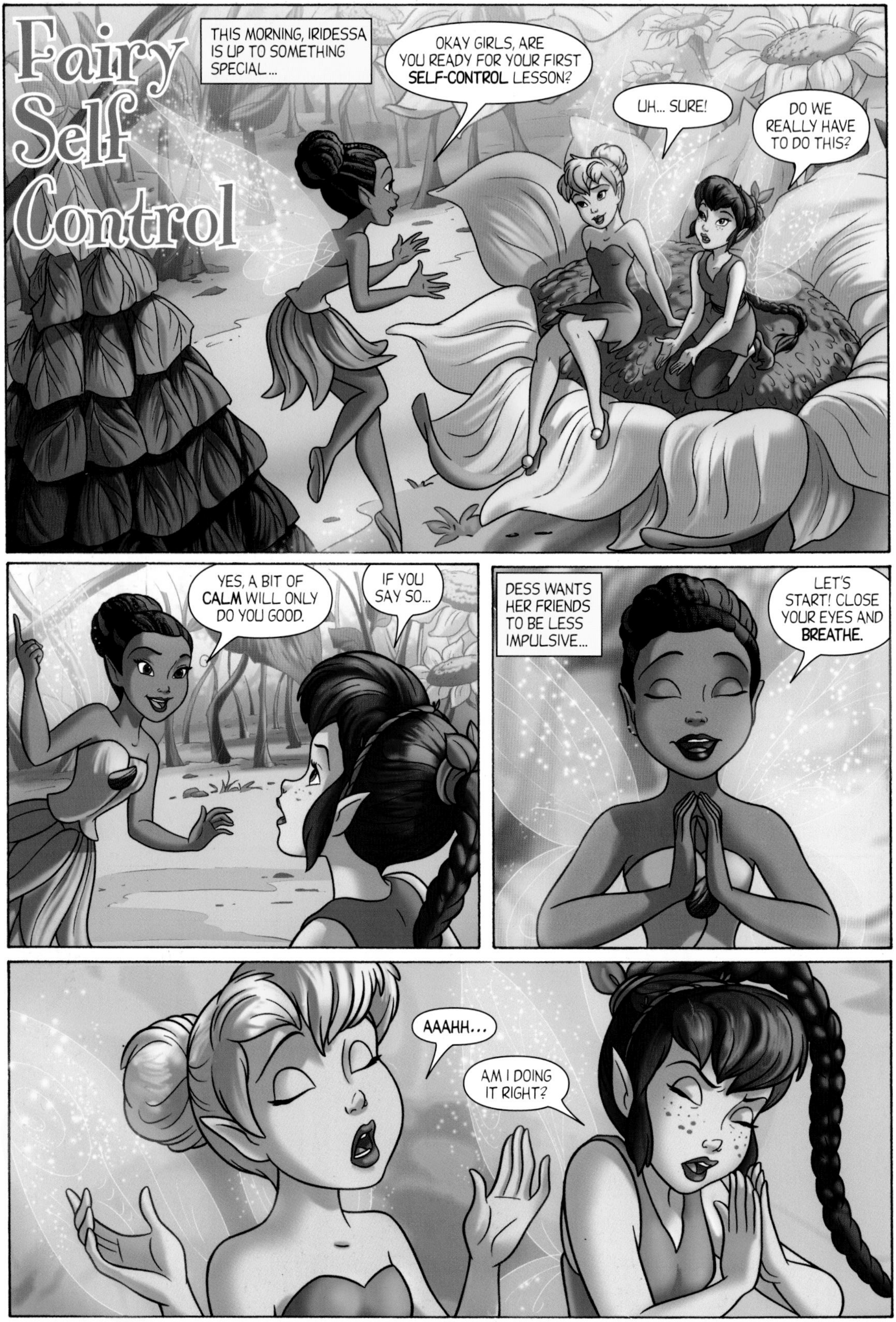
Fairy Self Control
THIS MORNING, IRIDESSA IS UP TO SOMETHING SPECIAL...
OKAY GIRLS, ARE YOU READY FOR YOUR FIRST SELF-CONTROL LESSON?
UH... SURE!
DO WE REALLY HAVE TO DO THIS?
YES, A BIT OF CALM WILL ONLY DO YOU GOOD.
IF YOU SAY SO...
DESS WANTS HER FRIENDS TO BE LESS IMPULSIVE...
LET'S START! CLOSE YOUR EYES AND BREATHE.
AAAHH...
AM I DOING IT RIGHT?

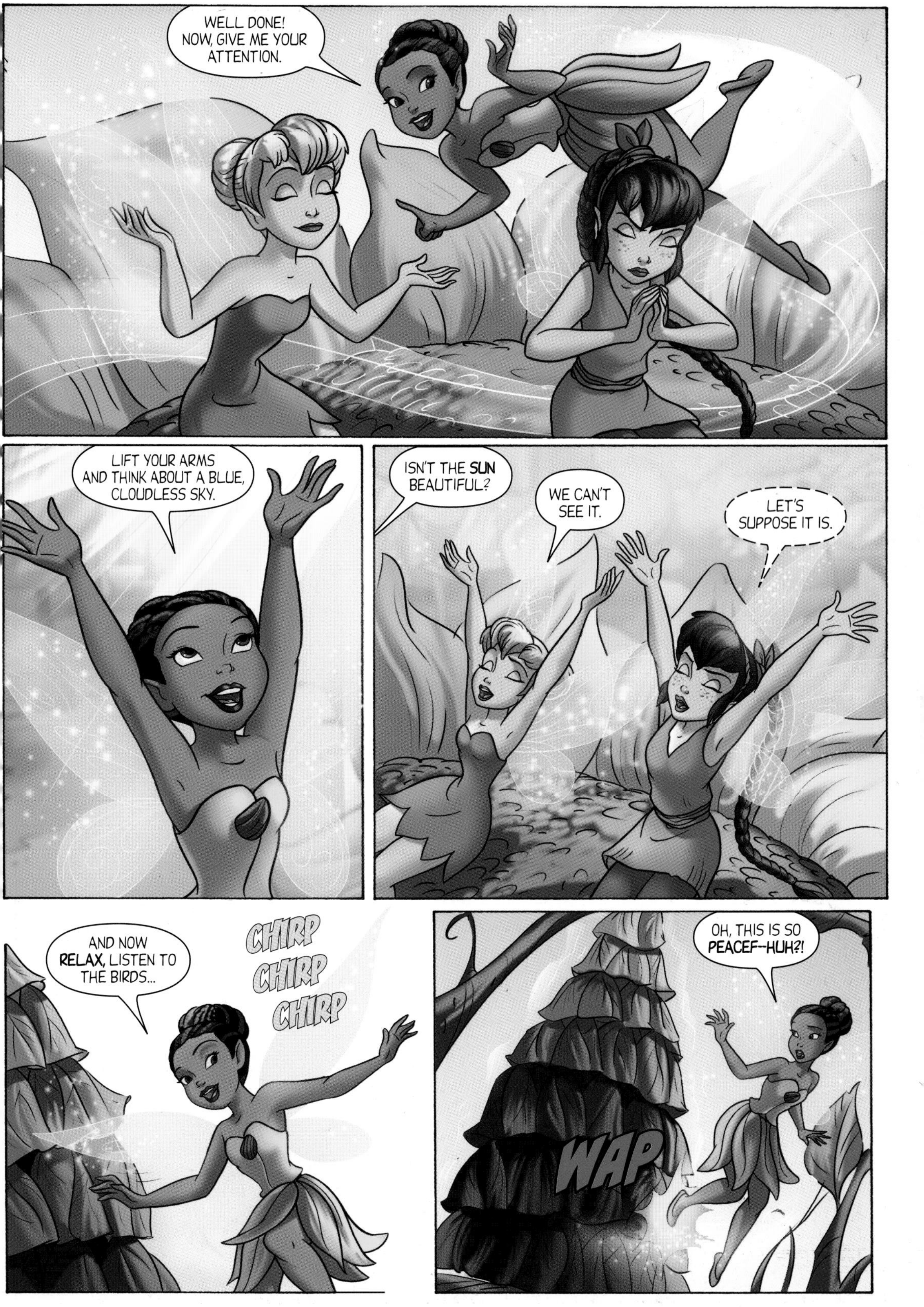
WELL DONE! NOW, GIVE ME YOUR ATTENTION.
LIFT YOUR ARMS AND THINK ABOUT A BLUE, CLOUDLESS SKY.
ISN'T THE **SUN** BEAUTIFUL?
WE CAN'T SEE IT.
LET'S SUPPOSE IT IS.
AND NOW **RELAX**, LISTEN TO THE BIRDS...
CHIRP
CHIRP
CHIRP
OH, THIS IS SO **PEACEF--HUH?!**
WAP

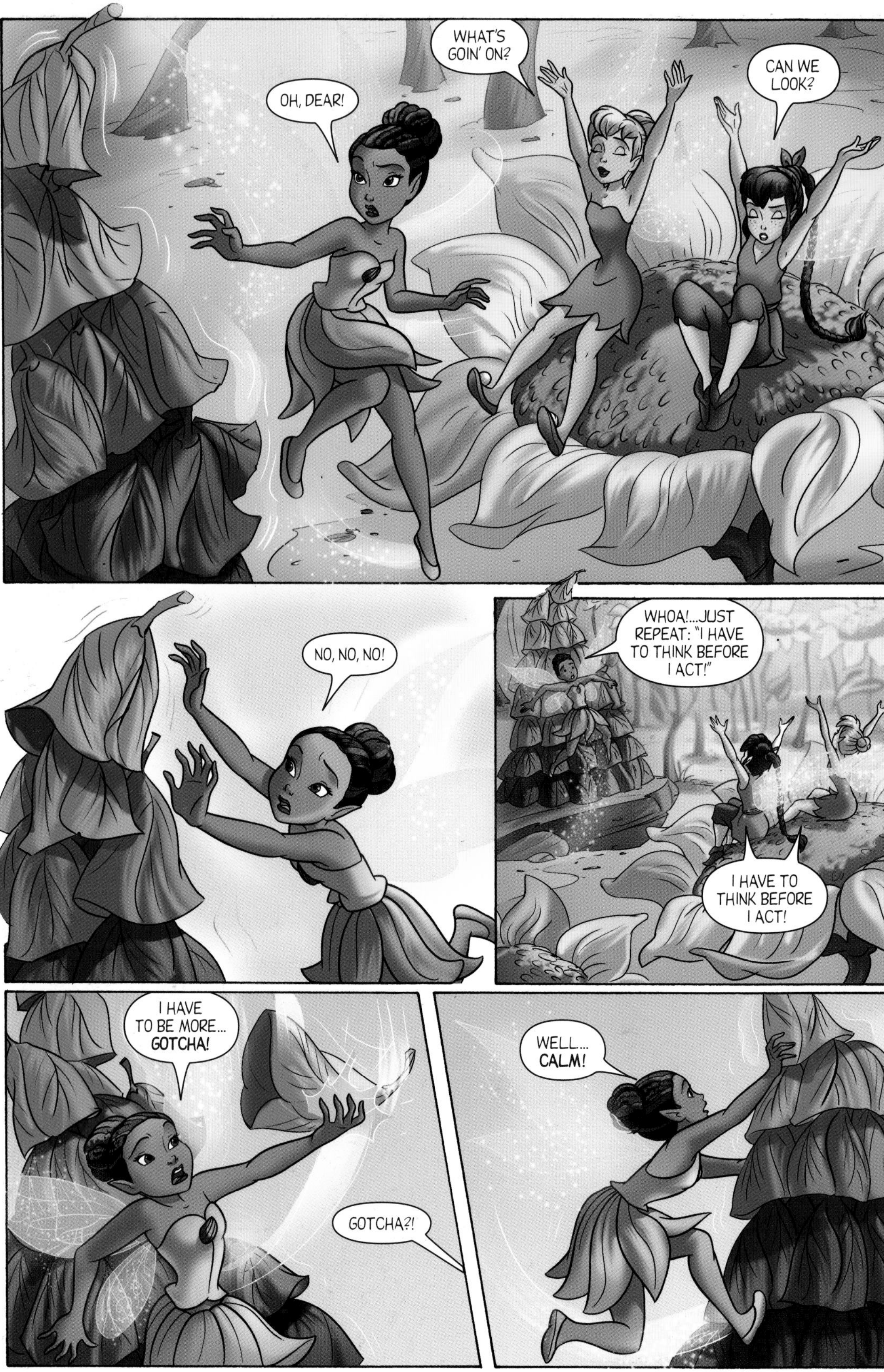
OH, DEAR!
WHAT'S GOIN' ON?
CAN WE LOOK?
NO, NO, NO!
WHOA!...JUST REPEAT: "I HAVE TO THINK BEFORE I ACT!"
I HAVE TO THINK BEFORE I ACT!
I HAVE TO BE MORE... **GOTCHA!**
GOTCHA?!
WELL... **CALM!**

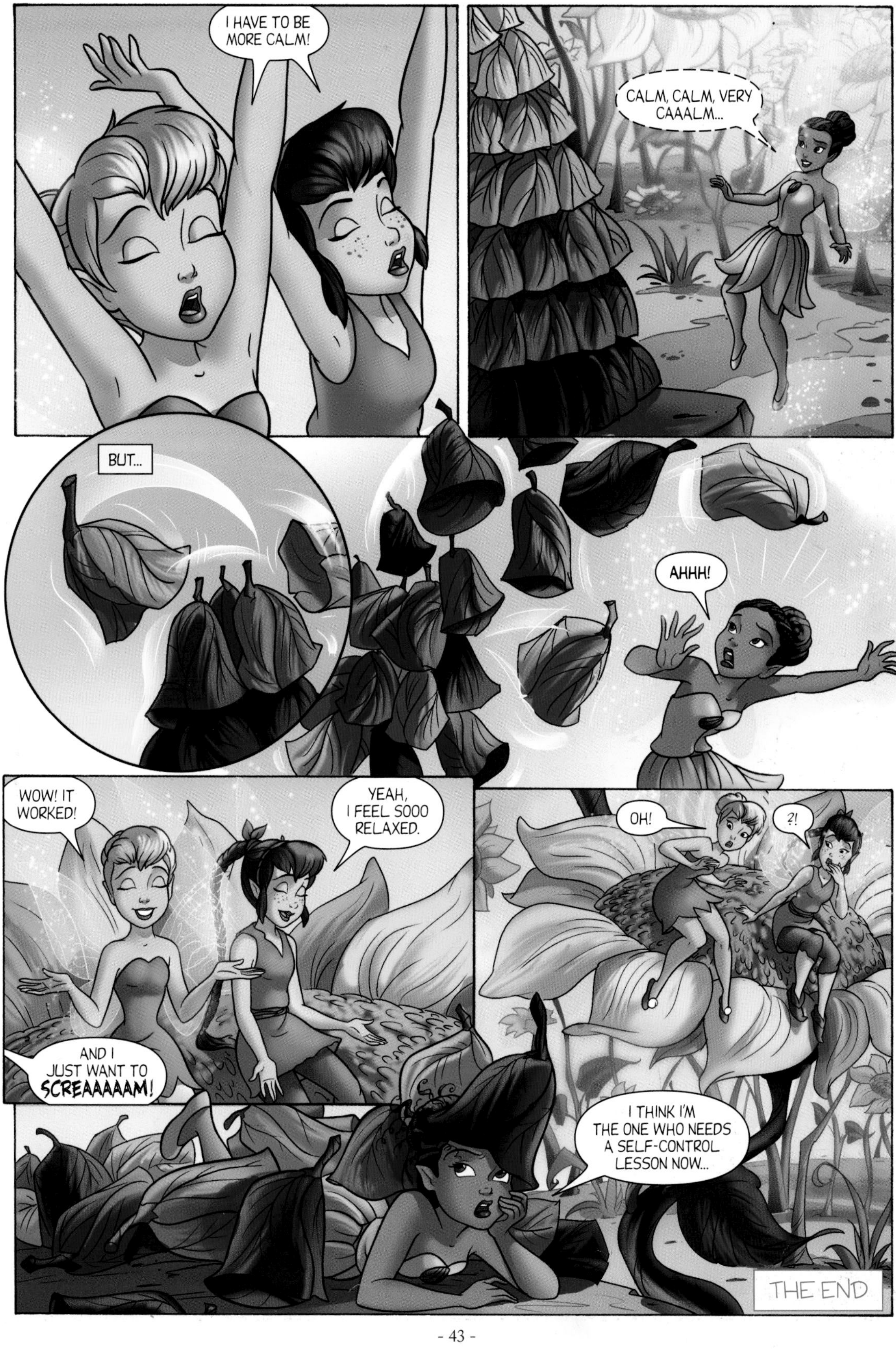

I HAVE TO BE MORE CALM!
CALM, CALM, VERY CAAALM...
BUT...
AHHH!
WOW! IT WORKED!
YEAH, I FEEL SOOO RELAXED.
AND I JUST WANT TO SCREAAAAAM!
OH!
?!
I THINK I'M THE ONE WHO NEEDS A SELF-CONTROL LESSON NOW...
THE END

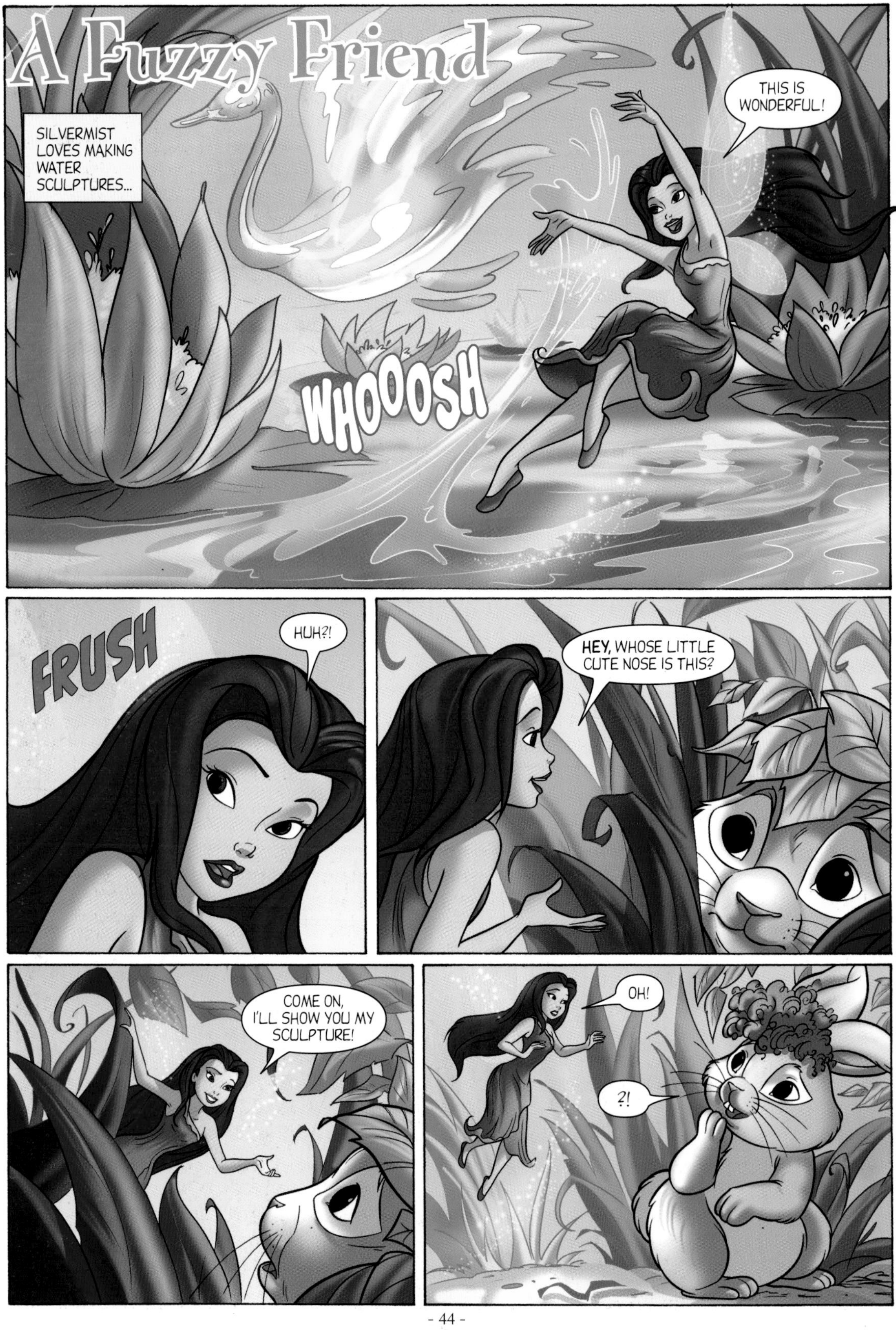
A Fuzzy Friend
SILVERMIST LOVES MAKING WATER SCULPTURES...
THIS IS WONDERFUL!
WHOOOSH
FRUSH
HUH?!
HEY, WHOSE LITTLE CUTE NOSE IS THIS?
COME ON, I'LL SHOW YOU MY SCULPTURE!
OH!
?!

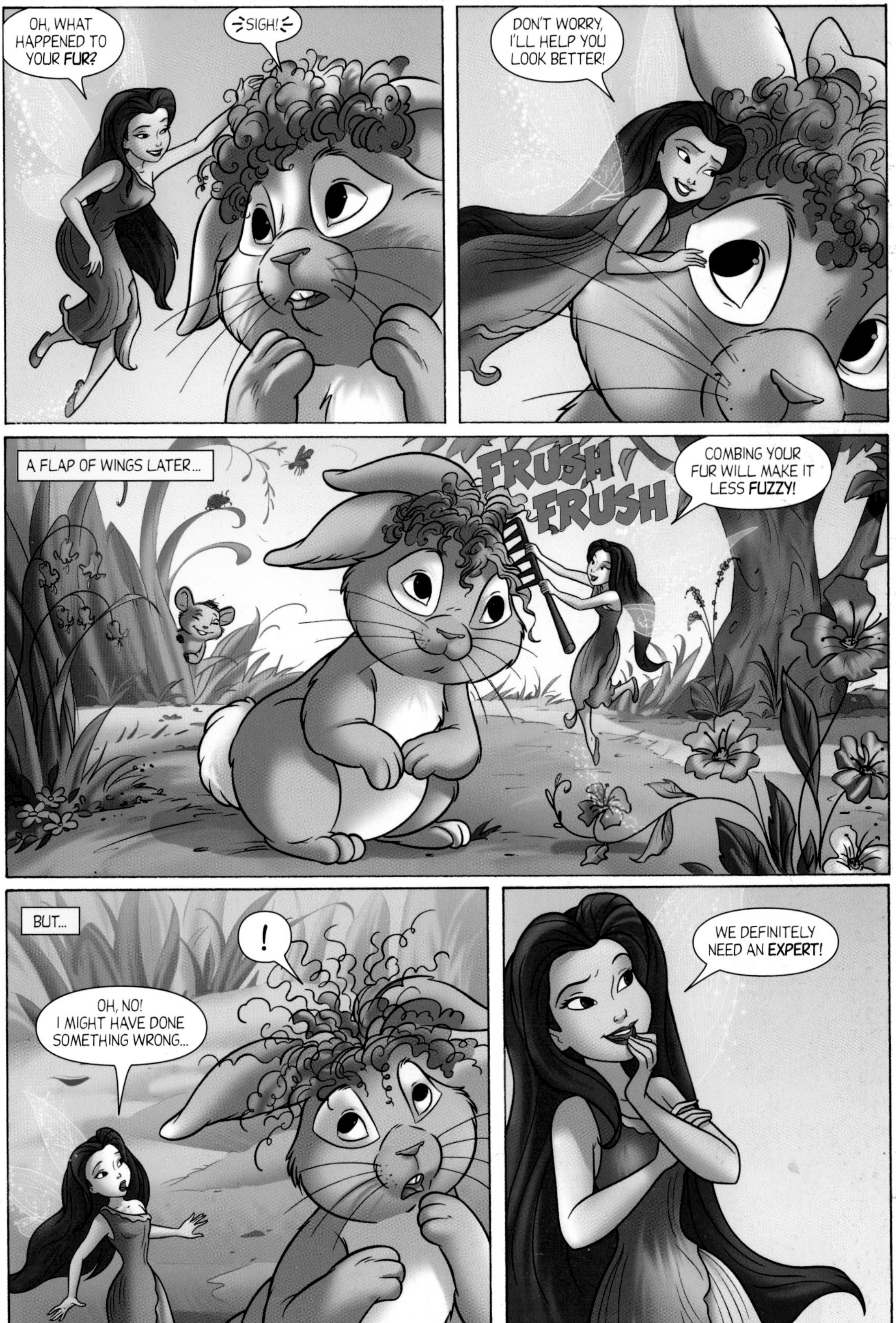
OH, WHAT HAPPENED TO YOUR FUR?
SIGH!
DON'T WORRY, I'LL HELP YOU LOOK BETTER!
A FLAP OF WINGS LATER...
FRUSH FRUSH
COMBING YOUR FUR WILL MAKE IT LESS FUZZY!
BUT...
!
OH, NO! I MIGHT HAVE DONE SOMETHING WRONG...
WE DEFINITELY NEED AN EXPERT!

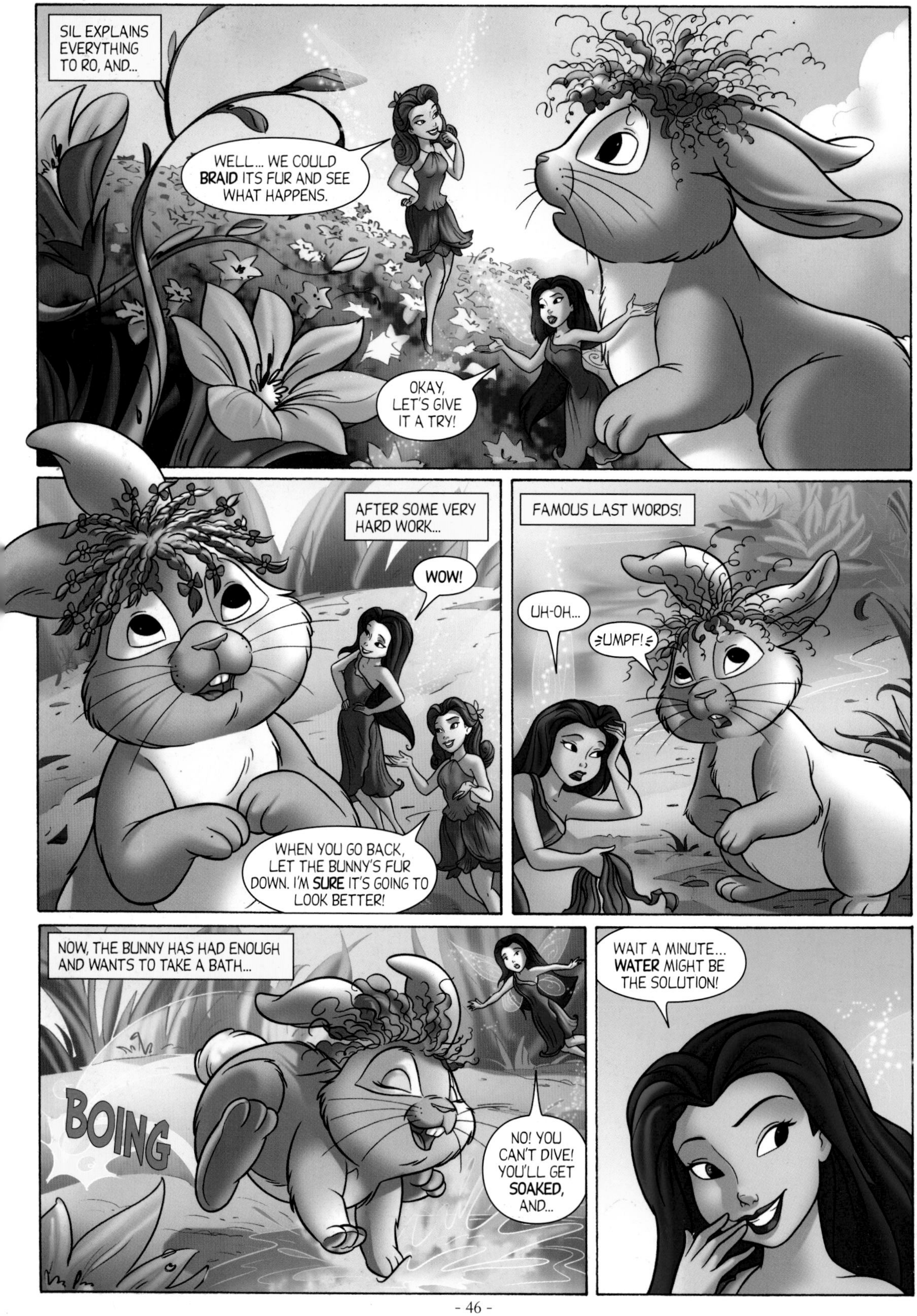
SIL EXPLAINS EVERYTHING TO RO, AND...
WELL... WE COULD **BRAID** ITS FUR AND SEE WHAT HAPPENS.
OKAY, LET'S GIVE IT A TRY!
AFTER SOME VERY HARD WORK...
WOW!
WHEN YOU GO BACK, LET THE BUNNY'S FUR DOWN. I'M **SURE** IT'S GOING TO LOOK BETTER!
FAMOUS LAST WORDS!
UH-OH...
UMPF!
NOW, THE BUNNY HAS HAD ENOUGH AND WANTS TO TAKE A BATH...
BOING
NO! YOU CAN'T DIVE! YOU'LL GET **SOAKED,** AND...
WAIT A MINUTE... **WATER** MIGHT BE THE SOLUTION!

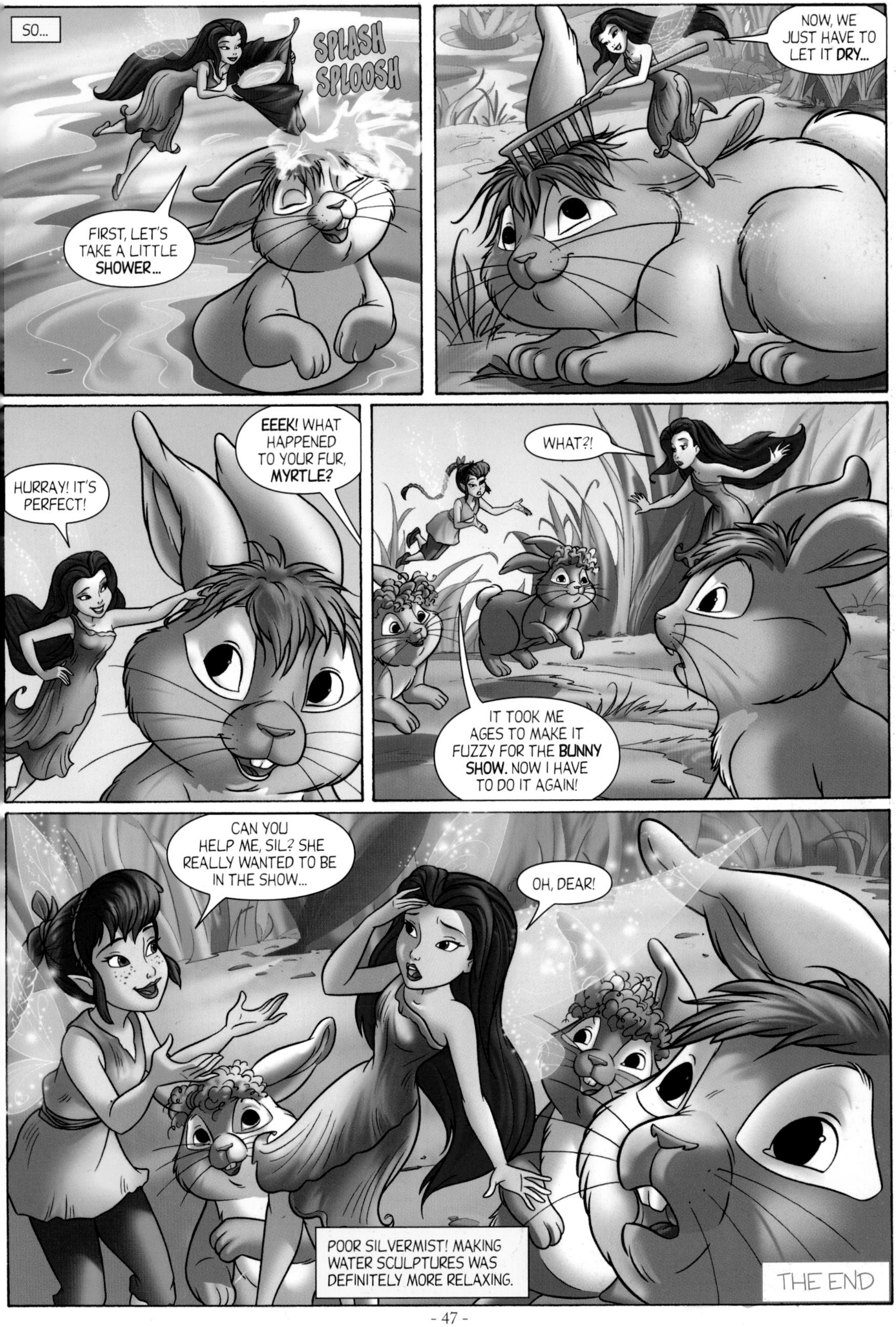
SO...
SPLASH SPLOOSH
FIRST, LET'S TAKE A LITTLE SHOWER...
NOW, WE JUST HAVE TO LET IT DRY...
HURRAY! IT'S PERFECT!
EEEK! WHAT HAPPENED TO YOUR FUR, MYRTLE?
WHAT?!
IT TOOK ME AGES TO MAKE IT FUZZY FOR THE BUNNY SHOW. NOW I HAVE TO DO IT AGAIN!
CAN YOU HELP ME, SIL? SHE REALLY WANTED TO BE IN THE SHOW...
OH, DEAR!
POOR SILVERMIST! MAKING WATER SCULPTURES WAS DEFINITELY MORE RELAXING.
THE END

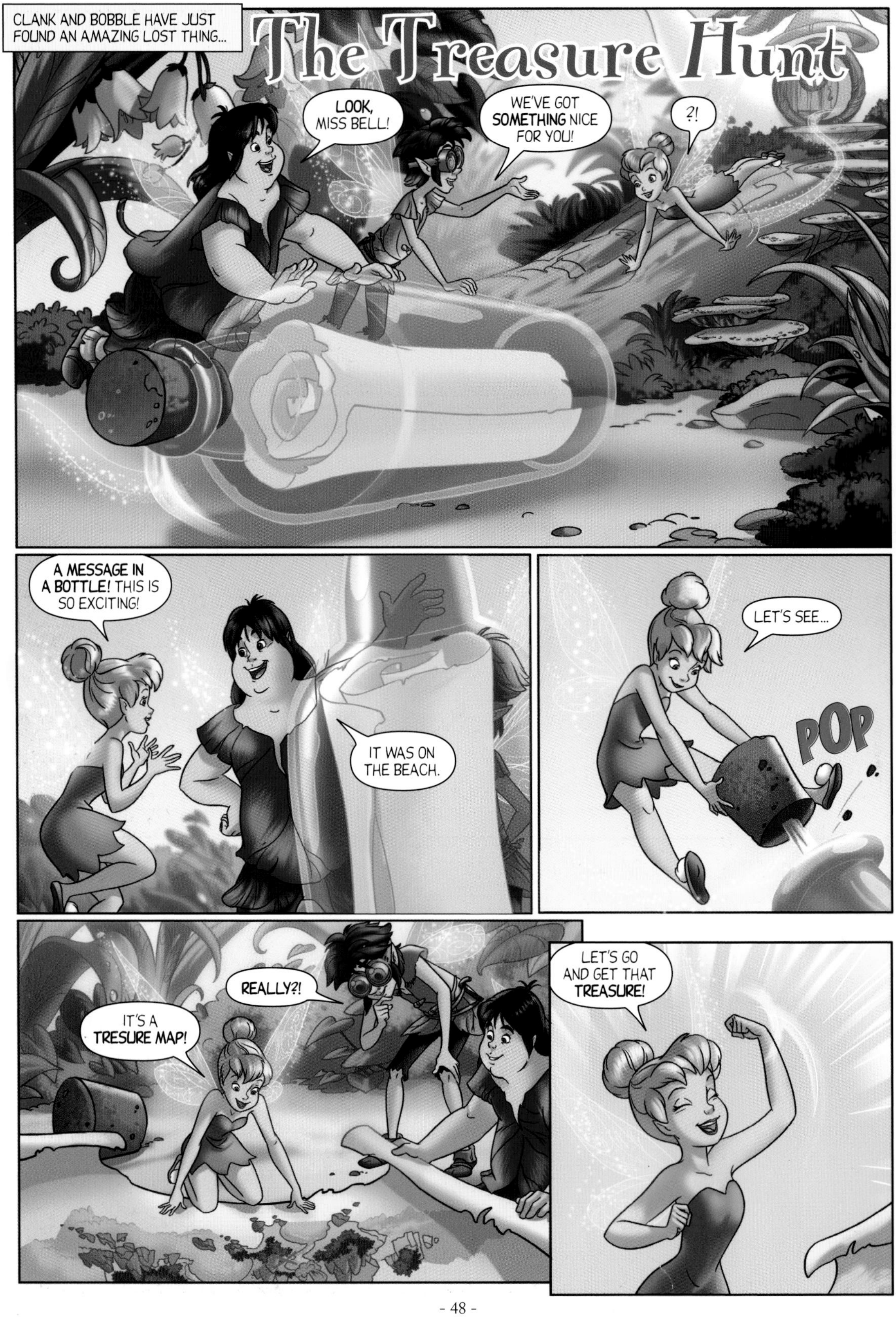
CLANK AND BOBBLE HAVE JUST FOUND AN AMAZING LOST THING...
The Treasure Hunt
LOOK, MISS BELL!
WE'VE GOT SOMETHING NICE FOR YOU!
?!
A MESSAGE IN A BOTTLE! THIS IS SO EXCITING!
IT WAS ON THE BEACH.
LET'S SEE...
POP
IT'S A TRESURE MAP!
REALLY?!
LET'S GO AND GET THAT TREASURE!

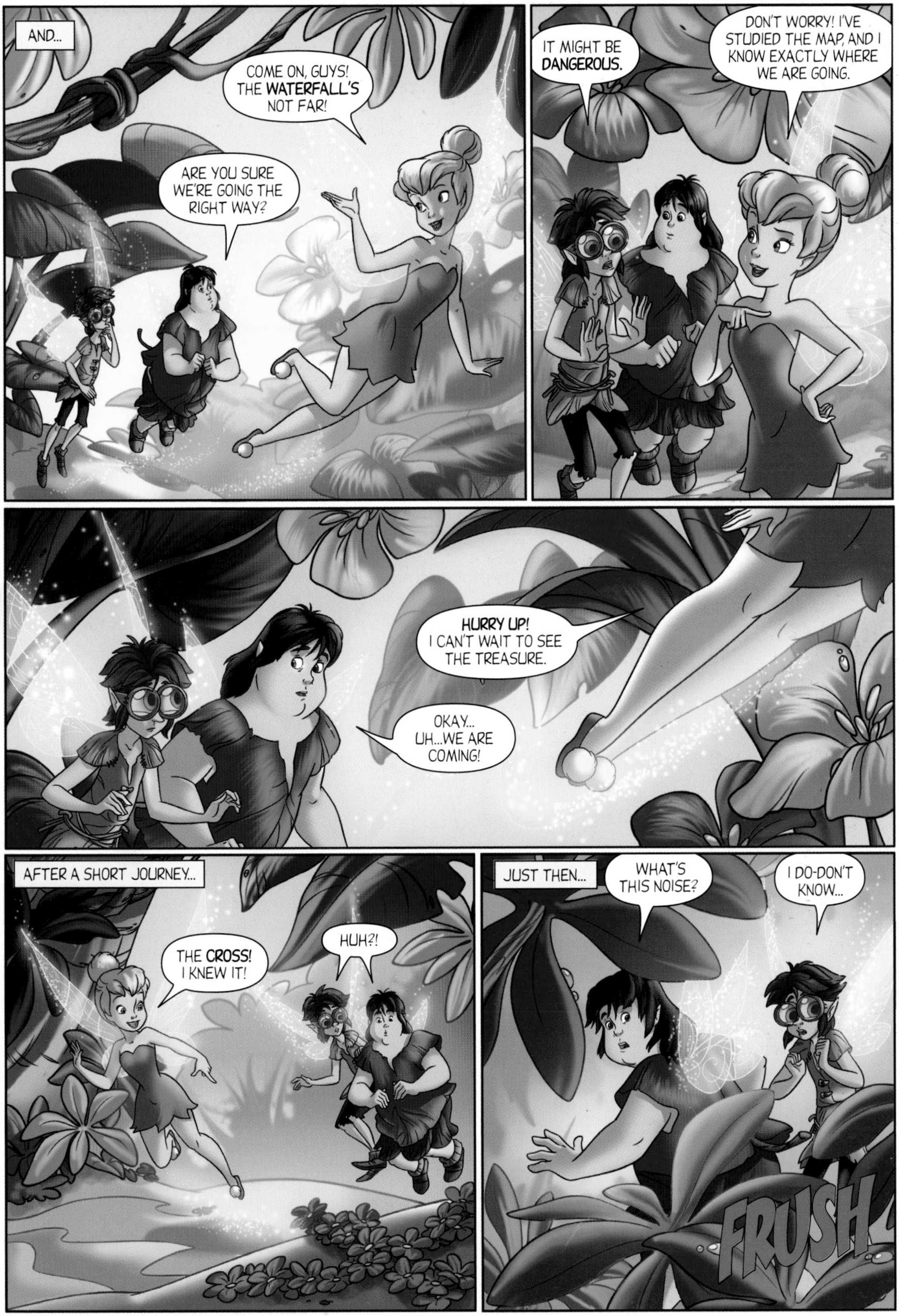
AND...
COME ON, GUYS! THE WATERFALL'S NOT FAR!
ARE YOU SURE WE'RE GOING THE RIGHT WAY?
IT MIGHT BE DANGEROUS.
DON'T WORRY! I'VE STUDIED THE MAP, AND I KNOW EXACTLY WHERE WE ARE GOING.
HURRY UP! I CAN'T WAIT TO SEE THE TREASURE.
OKAY... UH...WE ARE COMING!
AFTER A SHORT JOURNEY...
THE CROSS! I KNEW IT!
HUH?!
JUST THEN...
WHAT'S THIS NOISE?
I DO-DON'T KNOW...
FRUSH

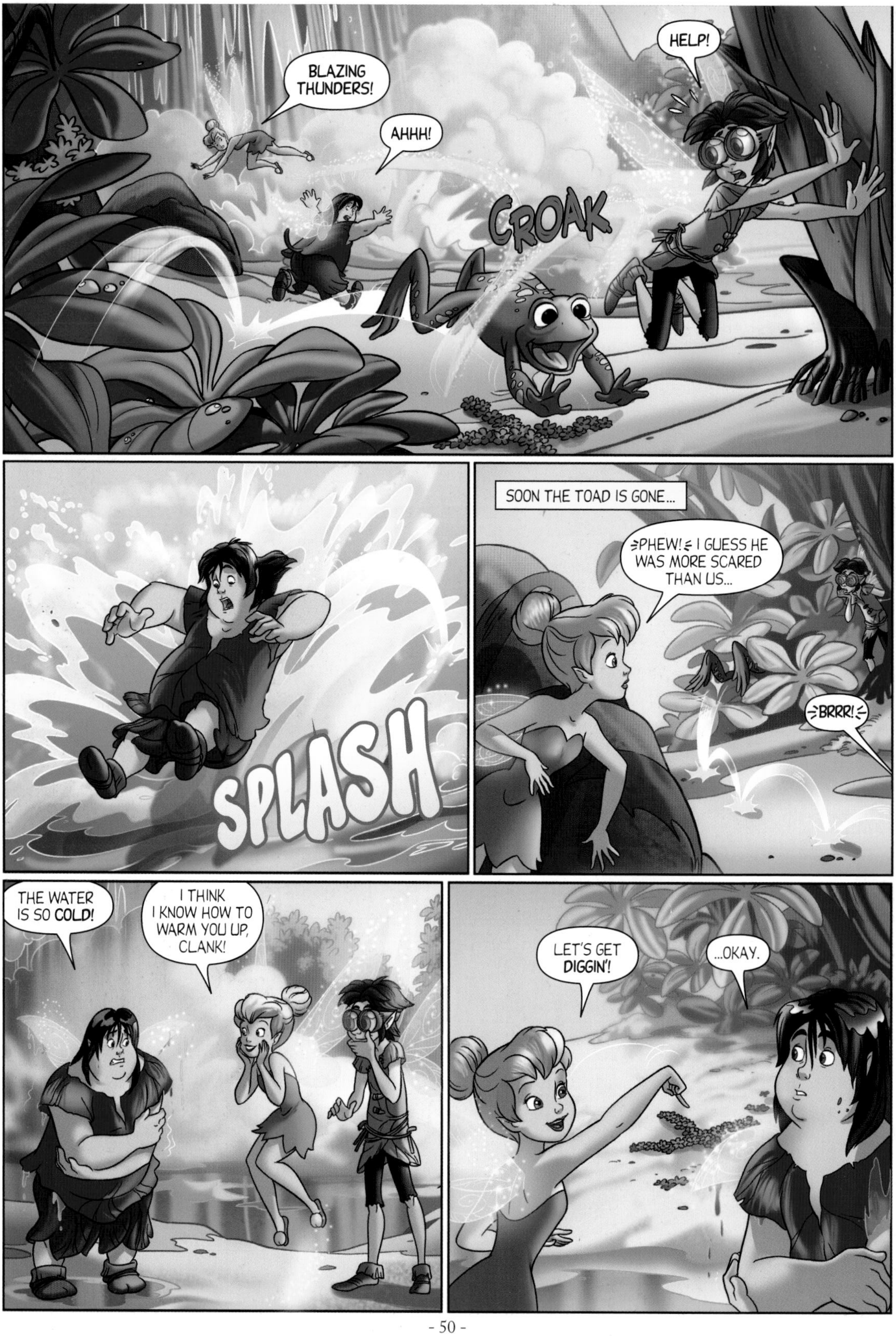
BLAZING THUNDERS!
AHHH!
HELP!
CROAK
SPLASH
SOON THE TOAD IS GONE...
PHEW! I GUESS HE WAS MORE SCARED THAN US...
BRRR!
THE WATER IS SO **COLD**!
I THINK I KNOW HOW TO WARM YOU UP, CLANK!
LET'S GET **DIGGIN'**!
...OKAY.

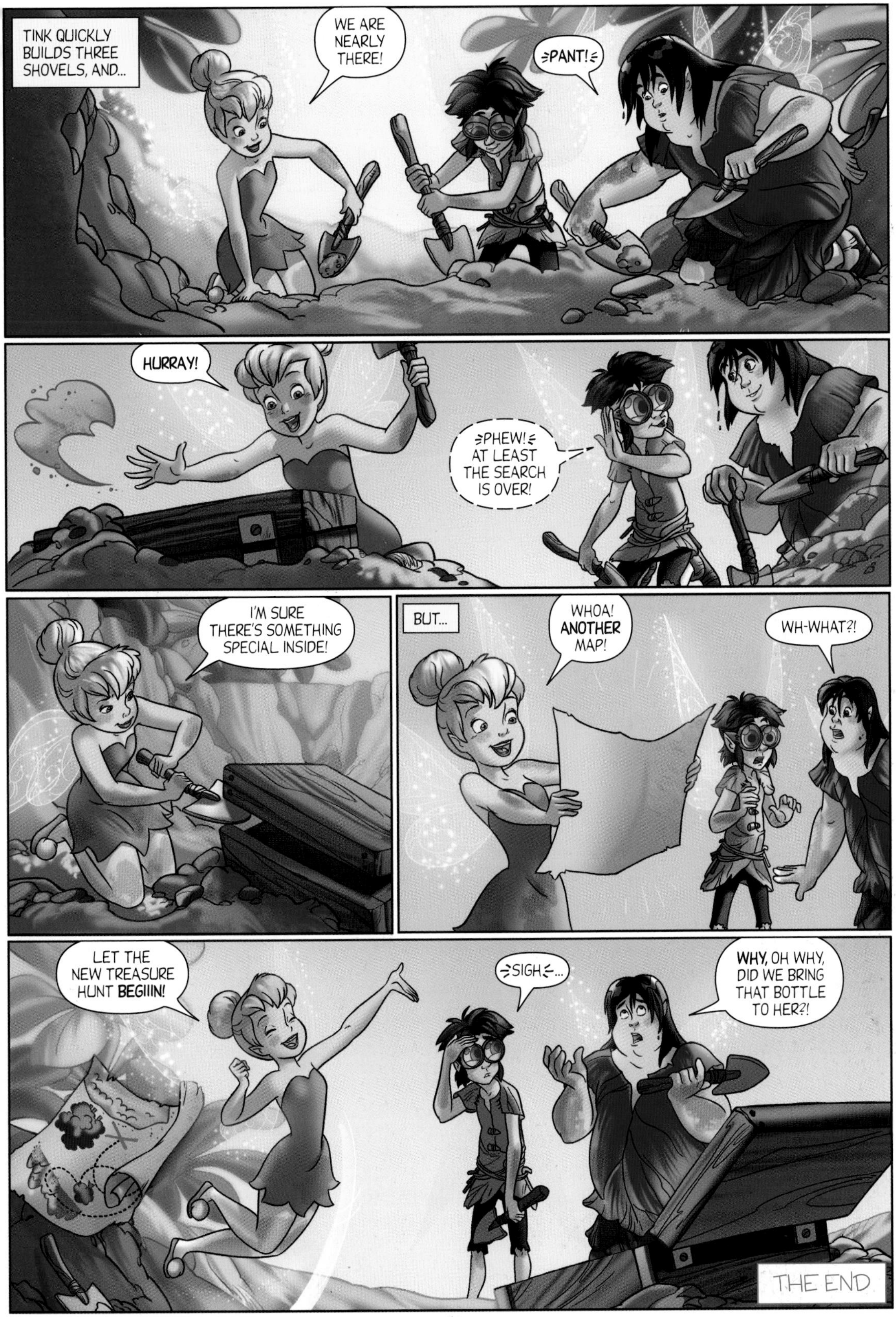

TINK QUICKLY BUILDS THREE SHOVELS, AND...
WE ARE NEARLY THERE!
PANT!
HURRAY!
PHEW! AT LEAST THE SEARCH IS OVER!
I'M SURE THERE'S SOMETHING SPECIAL INSIDE!
BUT...
WHOA! **ANOTHER** MAP!
WH-WHAT?!
LET THE NEW TREASURE HUNT **BEGIIIN!**
SIGH...
WHY, OH WHY, DID WE BRING THAT BOTTLE TO HER?!
THE END

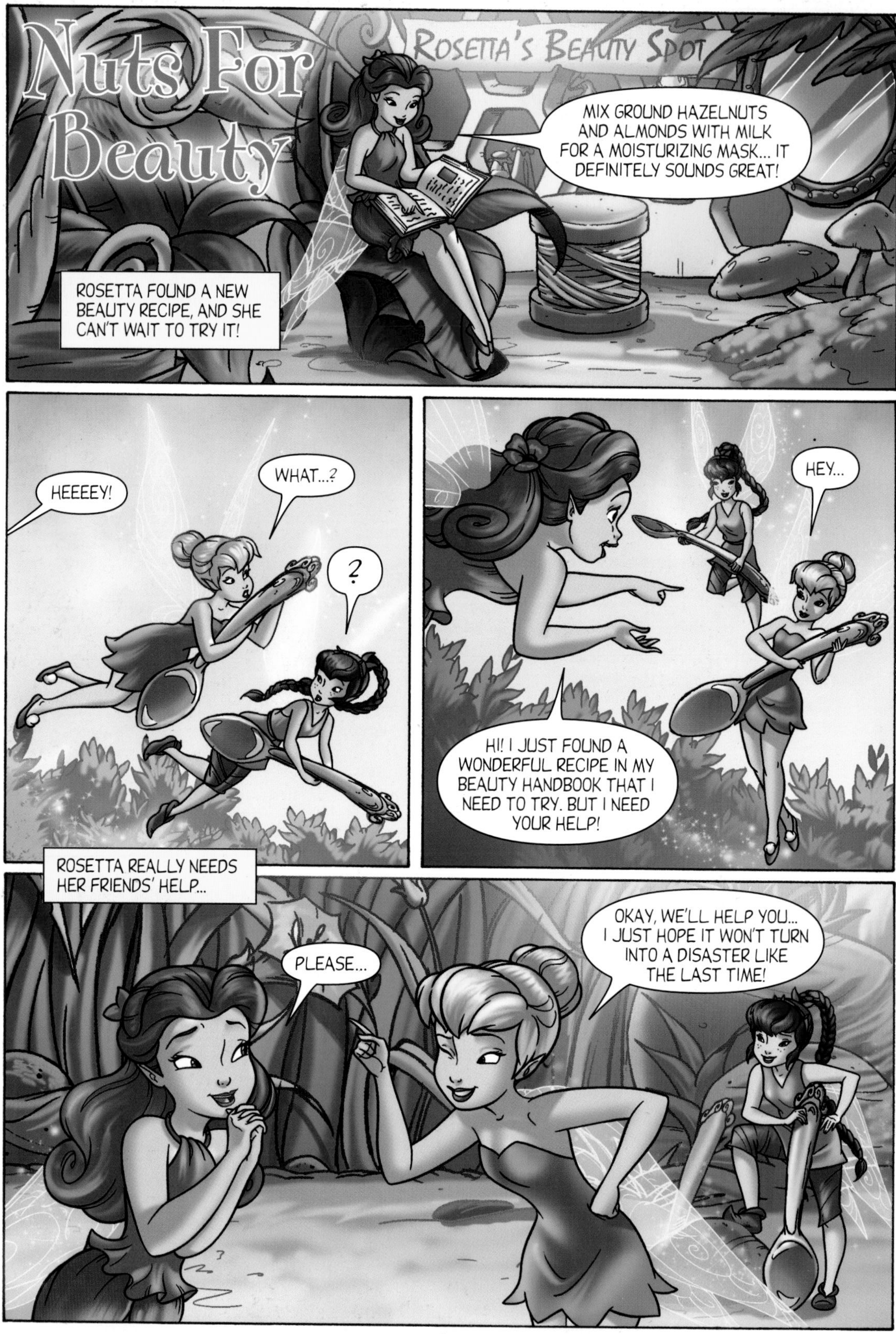

Nuts For Beauty
ROSETTA'S BEAUTY SPOT
MIX GROUND HAZELNUTS AND ALMONDS WITH MILK FOR A MOISTURIZING MASK... IT DEFINITELY SOUNDS GREAT!
ROSETTA FOUND A NEW BEAUTY RECIPE, AND SHE CAN'T WAIT TO TRY IT!
HEEEEY!
WHAT...?
?
HEY...
HI! I JUST FOUND A WONDERFUL RECIPE IN MY BEAUTY HANDBOOK THAT I NEED TO TRY. BUT I NEED YOUR HELP!
ROSETTA REALLY NEEDS HER FRIENDS' HELP...
PLEASE...
OKAY, WE'LL HELP YOU... I JUST HOPE IT WON'T TURN INTO A DISASTER LIKE THE LAST TIME!

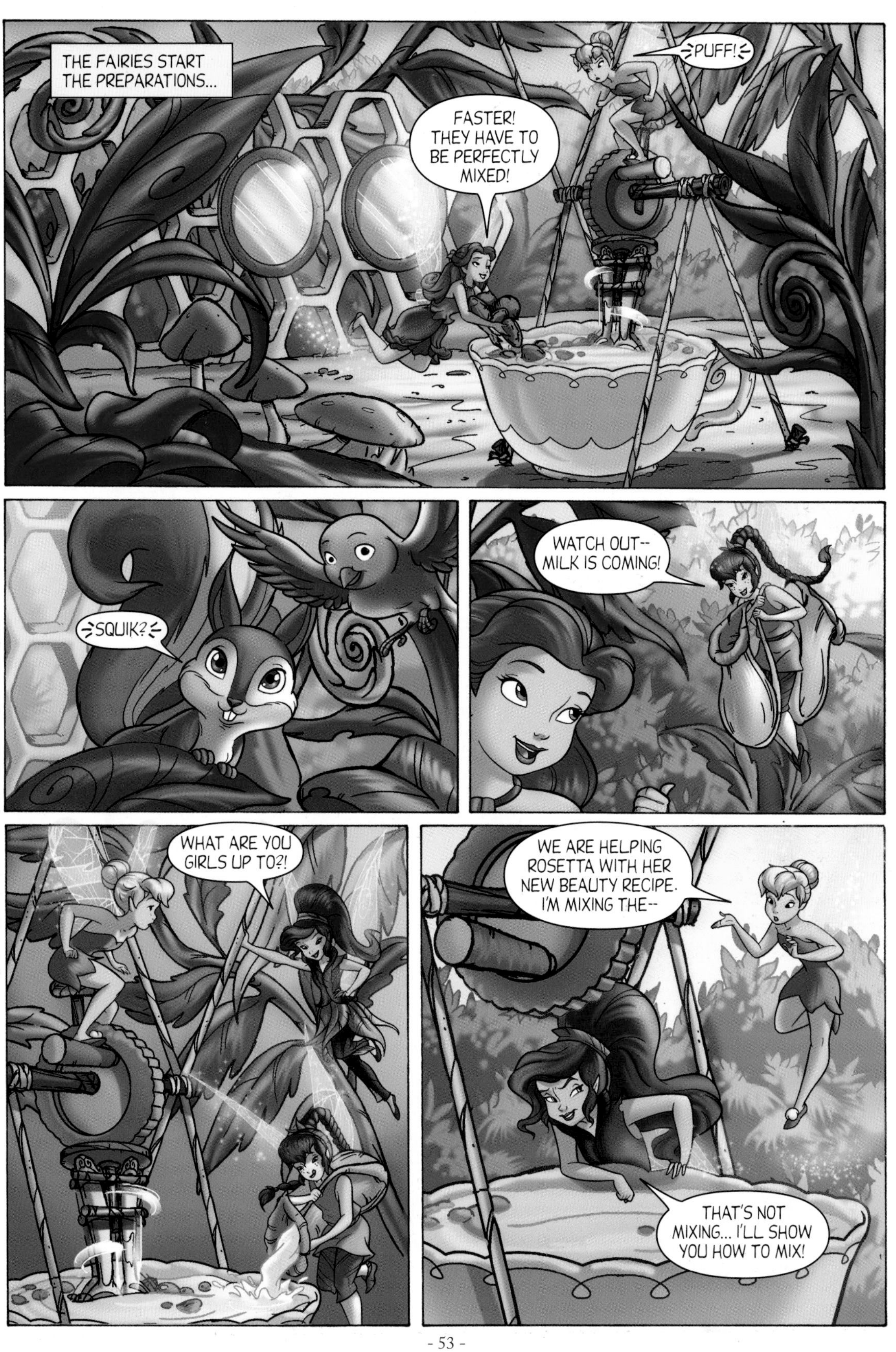
THE FAIRIES START THE PREPARATIONS...
PUFF!
FASTER! THEY HAVE TO BE PERFECTLY MIXED!
SQUIK?
WATCH OUT-- MILK IS COMING!
WHAT ARE YOU GIRLS UP TO?!
WE ARE HELPING ROSETTA WITH HER NEW BEAUTY RECIPE. I'M MIXING THE--
THAT'S NOT MIXING... I'LL SHOW YOU HOW TO MIX!

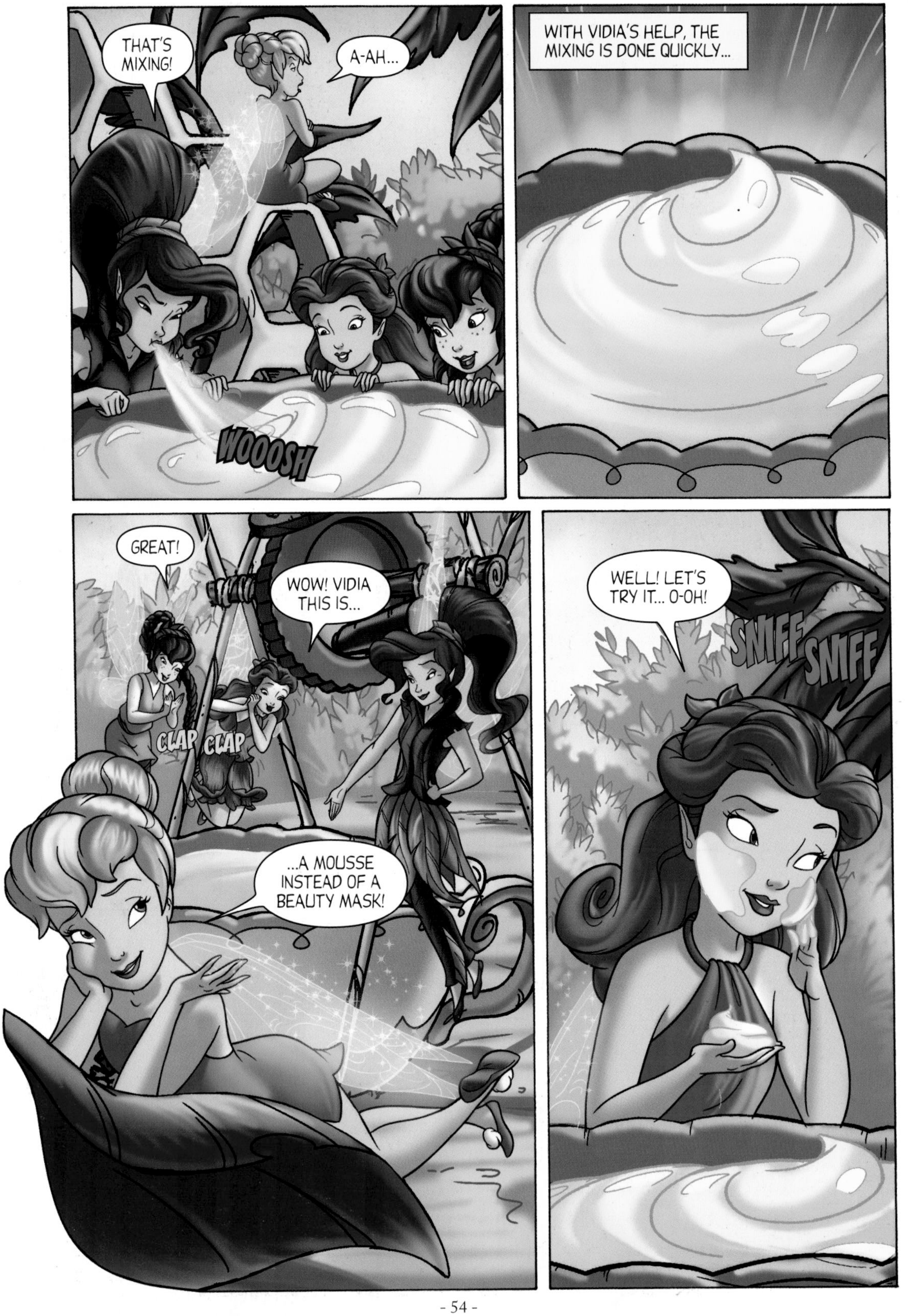
THAT'S MIXING!
A-AH...
WOOOSH
WITH VIDIA'S HELP, THE MIXING IS DONE QUICKLY...
GREAT!
WOW! VIDIA THIS IS...
CLAP CLAP
...A MOUSSE INSTEAD OF A BEAUTY MASK!
WELL! LET'S TRY IT... O-OH!
SNIFF SNIFF

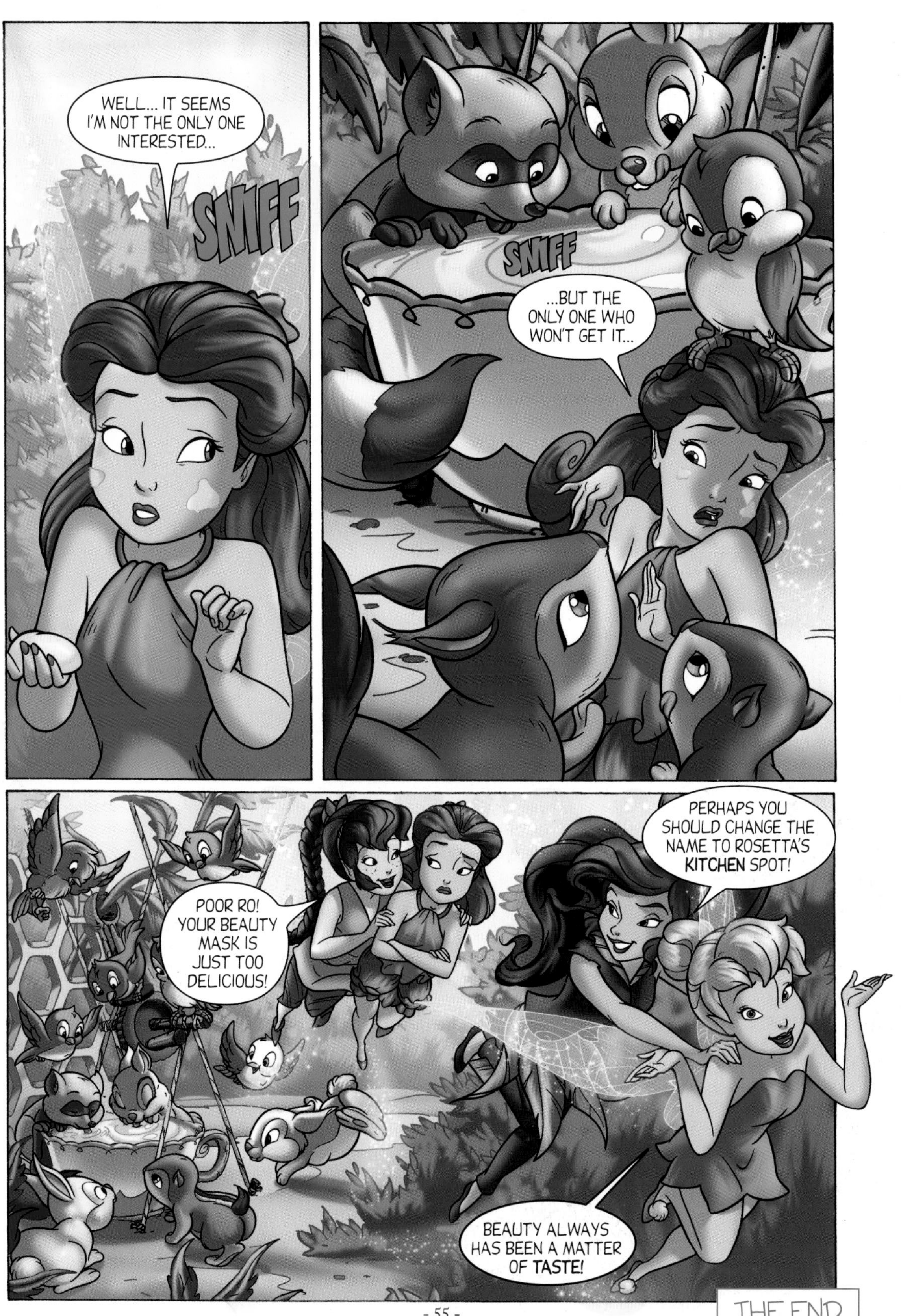

WELL... IT SEEMS I'M NOT THE ONLY ONE INTERESTED...
SNIFF
SNIFF
...BUT THE ONLY ONE WHO WON'T GET IT...
POOR RO! YOUR BEAUTY MASK IS JUST TOO DELICIOUS!
PERHAPS YOU SHOULD CHANGE THE NAME TO ROSETTA'S **KITCHEN** SPOT!
BEAUTY ALWAYS HAS BEEN A MATTER OF **TASTE**!

THE END

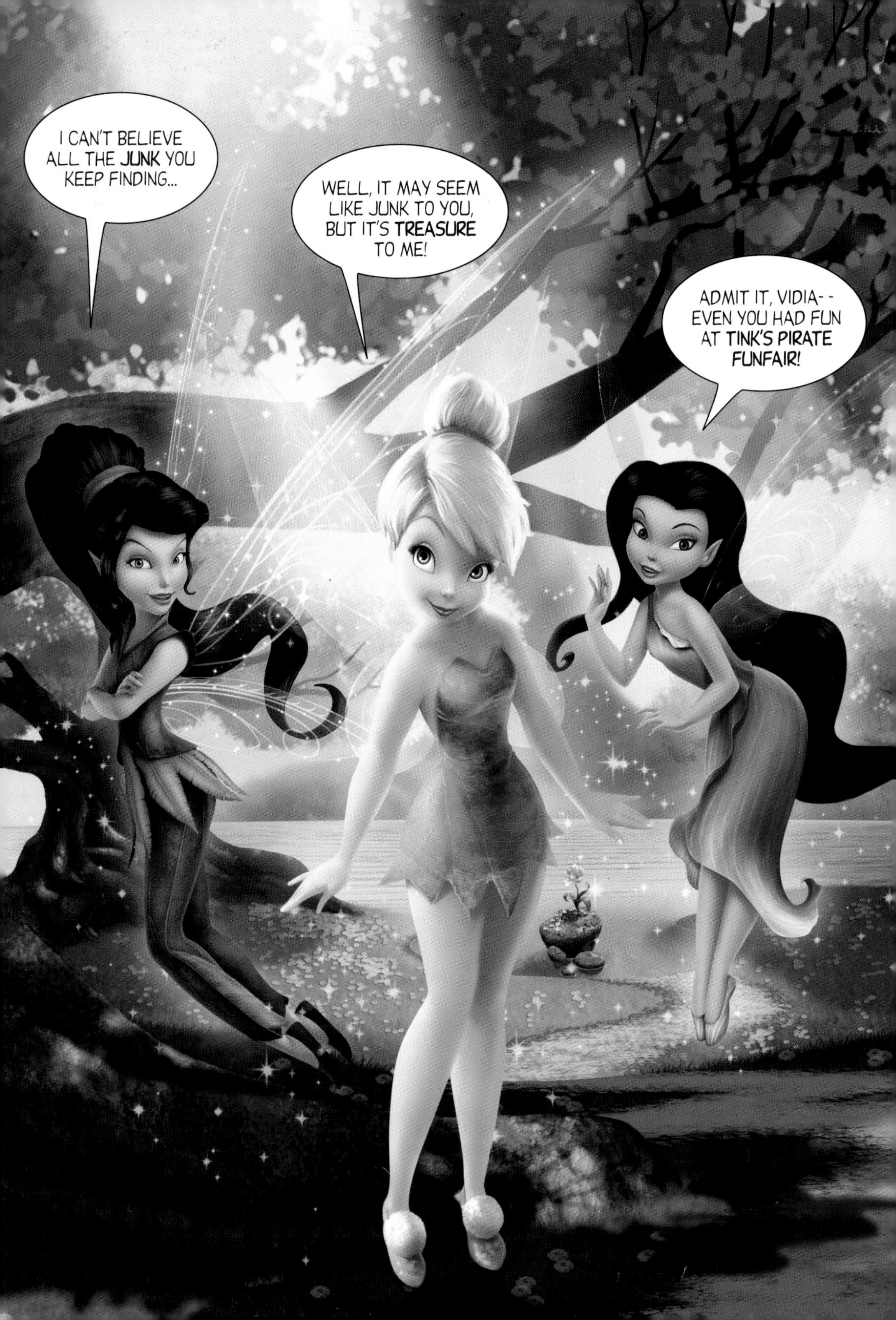
I CAN'T BELIEVE ALL THE **JUNK** YOU KEEP FINDING...
WELL, IT MAY SEEM LIKE JUNK TO YOU, BUT IT'S **TREASURE** TO ME!
ADMIT IT, VIDIA-- EVEN YOU HAD FUN AT **TINK'S PIRATE FUNFAIR!**

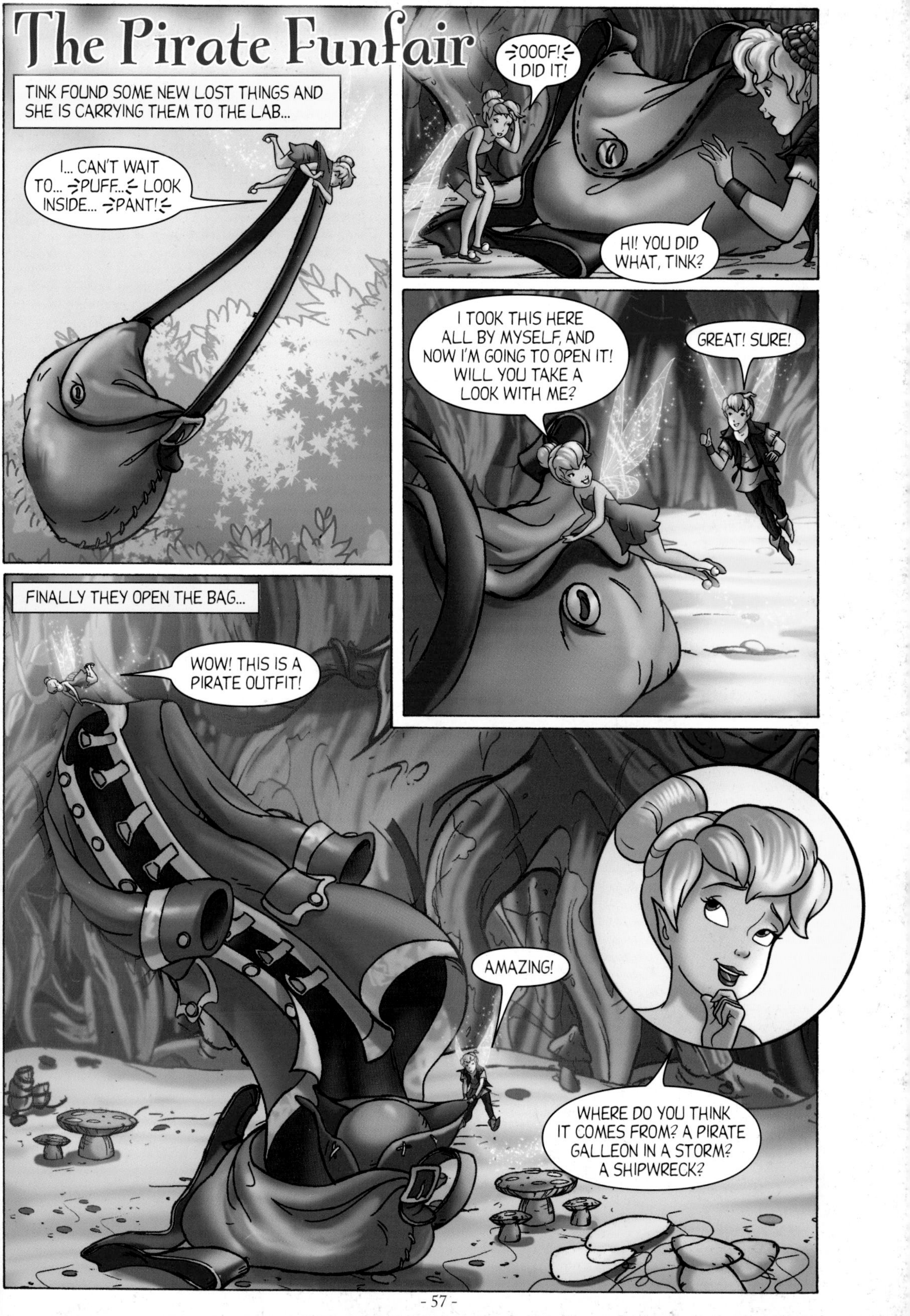
The Pirate Funfair
TINK FOUND SOME NEW LOST THINGS AND SHE IS CARRYING THEM TO THE LAB...
I... CAN'T WAIT TO... PUFF... LOOK INSIDE... PANT!
OOOF! I DID IT!
HI! YOU DID WHAT, TINK?
I TOOK THIS HERE ALL BY MYSELF, AND NOW I'M GOING TO OPEN IT! WILL YOU TAKE A LOOK WITH ME?
GREAT! SURE!
FINALLY THEY OPEN THE BAG...
WOW! THIS IS A PIRATE OUTFIT!
AMAZING!
WHERE DO YOU THINK IT COMES FROM? A PIRATE GALLEON IN A STORM? A SHIPWRECK?

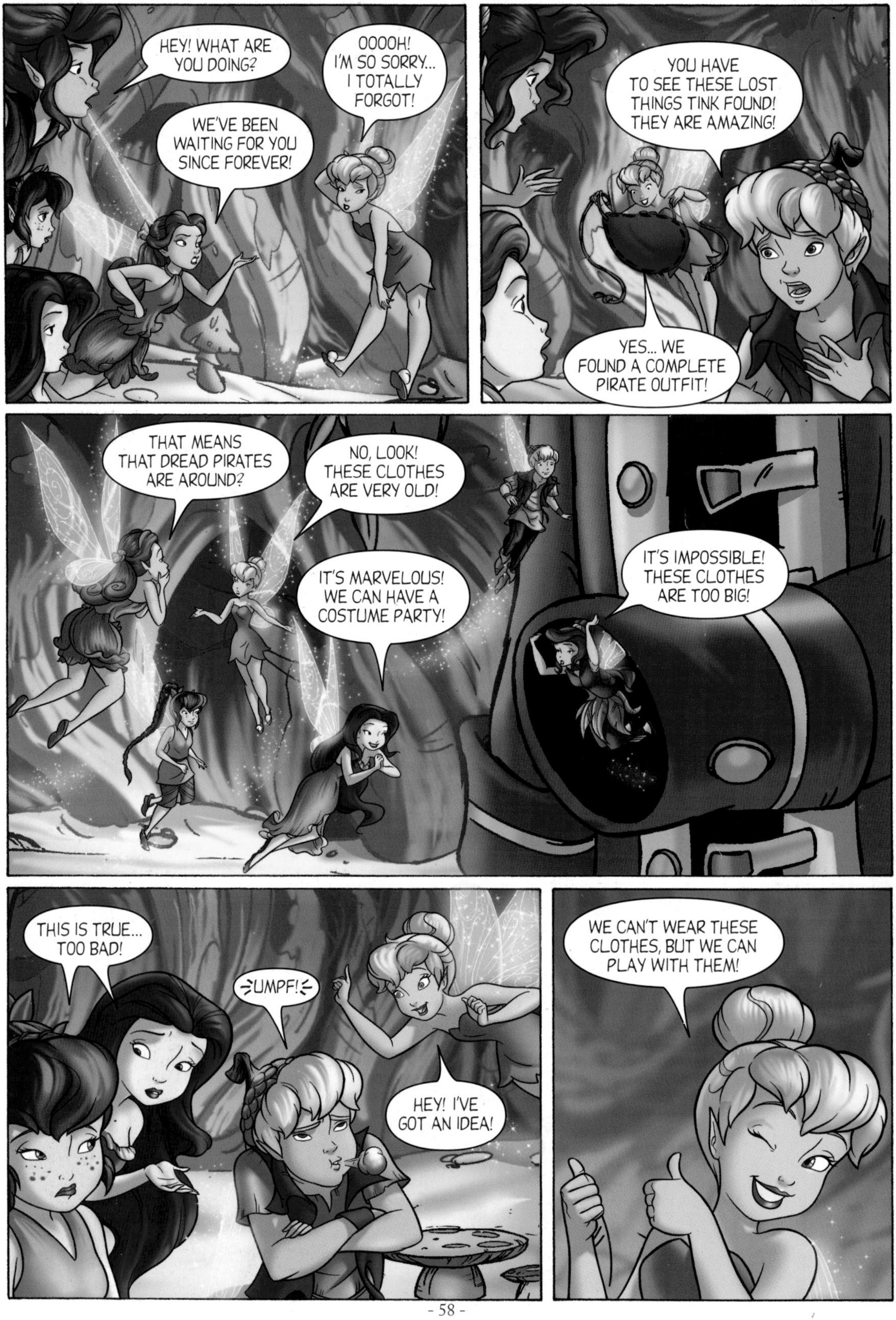
HEY! WHAT ARE YOU DOING?
WE'VE BEEN WAITING FOR YOU SINCE FOREVER!
OOOOH! I'M SO SORRY... I TOTALLY FORGOT!
YOU HAVE TO SEE THESE LOST THINGS TINK FOUND! THEY ARE AMAZING!
YES... WE FOUND A COMPLETE PIRATE OUTFIT!
THAT MEANS THAT DREAD PIRATES ARE AROUND?
NO, LOOK! THESE CLOTHES ARE VERY OLD!
IT'S MARVELOUS! WE CAN HAVE A COSTUME PARTY!
IT'S IMPOSSIBLE! THESE CLOTHES ARE TOO BIG!
THIS IS TRUE... TOO BAD!
UMPF!
HEY! I'VE GOT AN IDEA!
WE CAN'T WEAR THESE CLOTHES, BUT WE CAN PLAY WITH THEM!

TINK KNOWS WHAT TO DO, AND EVERY FAIRY IS READY TO WORK...

TERENCE, YOU FIND A BIKE WHEEL. RO, FETCH LOTS OF YARN! SIL, FIND CLOTHES PINS, AND VIDIA, COME WITH ME. WE HAVE TO FIND THAT WOODEN THING I FOUND ONCE...

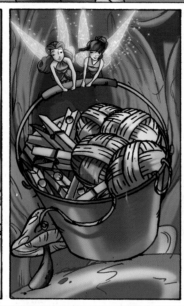

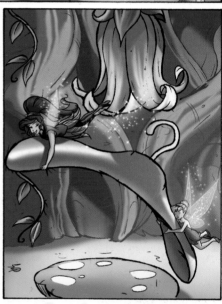

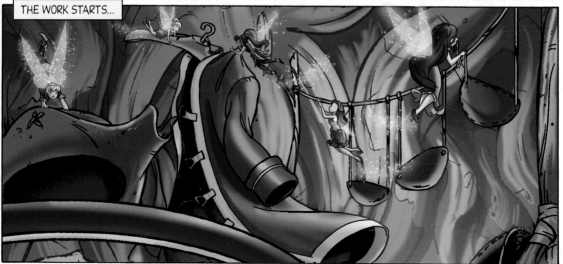

THE WORK STARTS...

- 59 -

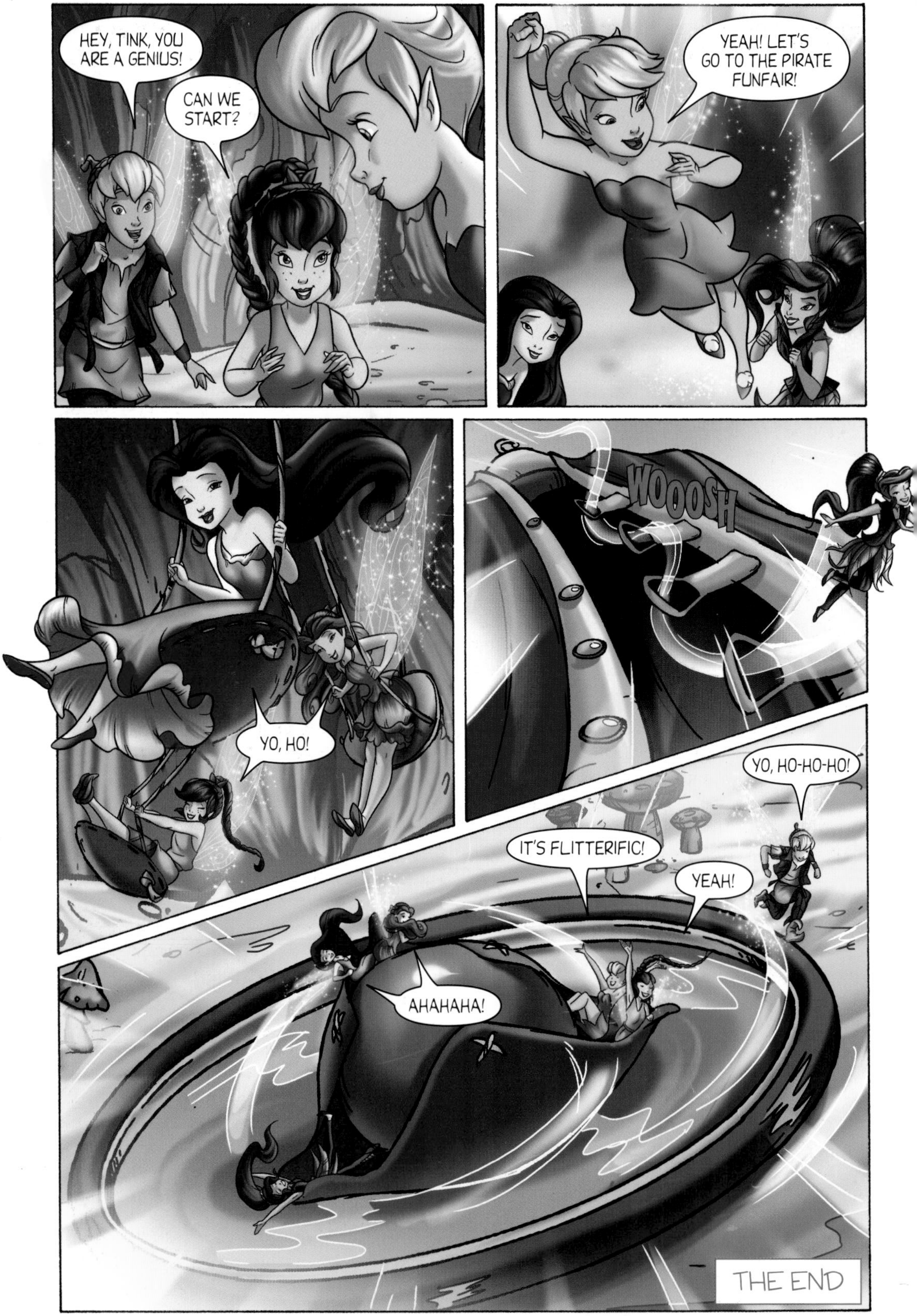
HEY, TINK, YOU ARE A GENIUS!
CAN WE START?
YEAH! LET'S GO TO THE PIRATE FUNFAIR!
YO, HO!
WOOOSH
YO, HO-HO-HO!
IT'S FLITTERIFIC!
YEAH!
AHAHAHA!
THE END

WATCH OUT FOR PAPERCUTZ

Welcome to the Never Land-centric nineteenth DISNEY FAIRIES graphic novel from Papercutz, those magical folk dedicated to publishing great graphic novels for all ages. I'm Jim Salicrup, the comicbook fairy who is here to let you know what other wonderful graphic novels we're publishing starring the delightful classic Disney superstars...

Disney
MINNIE & DAISY
BEST FRIENDS FOREVER
Disney COMICS
PAPERCUTZ

But before we get to that, I just have to marvel at the awesome amount of DISNEY FAIRIES characters we managed to squeeze into this enchanted graphic novel... There's Cheese, Tinker Bell (of course!), Fawn, Rosetta, Iridessa, Silvermist, Vidia, Clank, Bobble, Periwinkle, Fiona, Dewey, Fairy Mary, Sled, Baby Croc, and Terence! Talk about an all-star cast...! And even with all of that, we still have a little room left to give you a special preview of the MINNIE & DAISY "Best Friends Forever" graphic novel. How lucky can you get?

We're hoping that if you enjoy stories of Tinker Bell and all her fairy friends, that you'll also enjoy the fun-filled adventures of Minnie Mouse and Daisy Duck, back in their school days when they were BFFs. Starting on the very next page there's a very short sampling of comics from their debut Papercutz graphic novel that's available now from booksellers (and libraries) everywhere.

Speaking of Minnie Mouse, she has a cameo appearance in another Papercutz graphic novel that is just a little bit different. It's called GREAT PARODIES "Mickey's Inferno." This very special graphic novel features, for the very first time in the USA, an unabridged version of a truly classic Disney comic that was created in Italy in 1949. It features a spoof of one of Italy's, and the world's, greatest works of poetry, "The Divine Comedy," by Dante Alighieri, but in this version, after Mickey Mouse and Goofy appear as Dante and Virgil, they explore the various layers of Paradise and the Underworld. And if that's not strange enough, in addition to Minnie's cameo appearance, "Mickey's Inferno" also features appearances by Peg-Leg Pete, Morty the Mesmerist, Huey, Dewey, Louie, Pluto, Dumbo, Clarabelle, Br're Fox, Br're Bear, Dopey (in a rare speaking role!), Donald Duck, José Carioca, Panchito Pistoles, Geppetto, Doc, the Blue Fairy, Honest John, Gideon, Jiminy Cricket, Br'er Rabbit, Eega Beeva, Practical Pig, Fiddler Pig, Fifer Pig, Zeke Midas Wolf, Li'l Wolf, Pflip the Thnuckle-booh, and probably a few more that I didn't recognize! It's a great bit of Disney comics history as well as an original take on Dante's masterpiece! This is a must-have for serious animation and comic art lovers!

Disney
GREAT PARODIES MICKEY'S
INFERNO
Disney COMICS
PAPERCUTZ

We have even more exciting Disney comics news, but we're almost out of room. You can, however, visit www.papercutz.com and find out all the latest details. So, until we meet again, keep believing in "faith, trust, and pixie dust"!

Thanks,

Jim

STAY IN TOUCH!

EMAIL:	salicrup@papercutz.com
WEB:	papercutz.com
TWITTER:	@papercutzgn
FACEBOOK:	PAPERCUTZGRAPHICNOVELS
REGULAR MAIL:	Papercutz, 160 Broadway, Suite 700, East Wing, New York, NY 10038

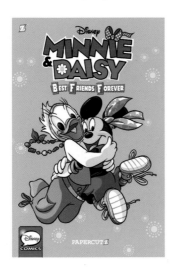

Special Preview of MINNIE & DAISY "Best Friends Forever"…

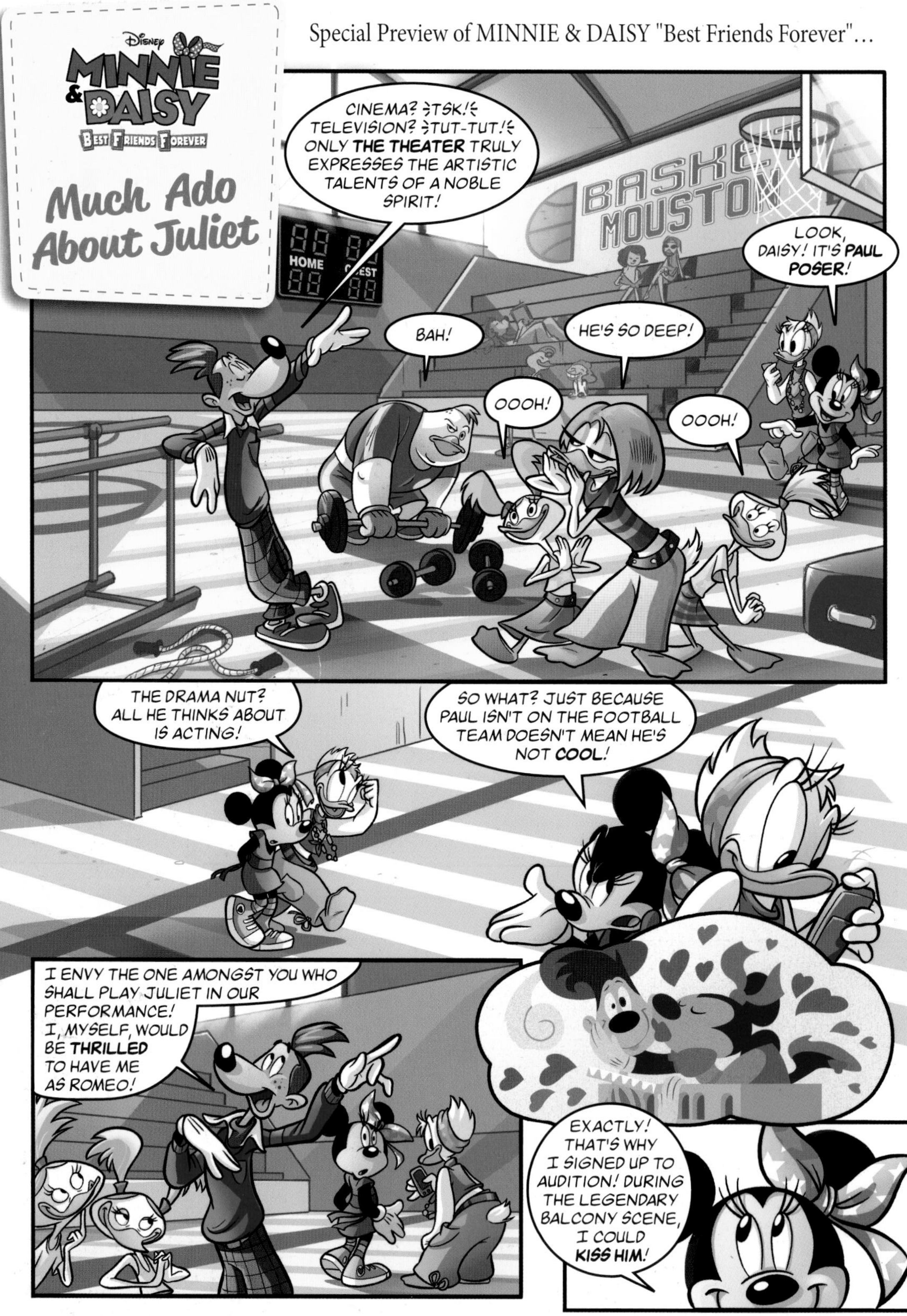

DISNEY
MINNIE & DAISY
BEST FRIENDS FOREVER
Much Ado About Juliet
CINEMA? ≑TSK!≑ TELEVISION? ≑TUT-TUT!≑ ONLY THE THEATER TRULY EXPRESSES THE ARTISTIC TALENTS OF A NOBLE SPIRIT!
BASKET MOUSTON
HOME
GUEST
LOOK, DAISY! IT'S PAUL POSER!
BAH!
HE'S SO DEEP!
OOOH!
OOOH!
THE DRAMA NUT? ALL HE THINKS ABOUT IS ACTING!
SO WHAT? JUST BECAUSE PAUL ISN'T ON THE FOOTBALL TEAM DOESN'T MEAN HE'S NOT COOL!
I ENVY THE ONE AMONGST YOU WHO SHALL PLAY JULIET IN OUR PERFORMANCE! I, MYSELF, WOULD BE THRILLED TO HAVE ME AS ROMEO!
EXACTLY! THAT'S WHY I SIGNED UP TO AUDITION! DURING THE LEGENDARY BALCONY SCENE, I COULD KISS HIM!

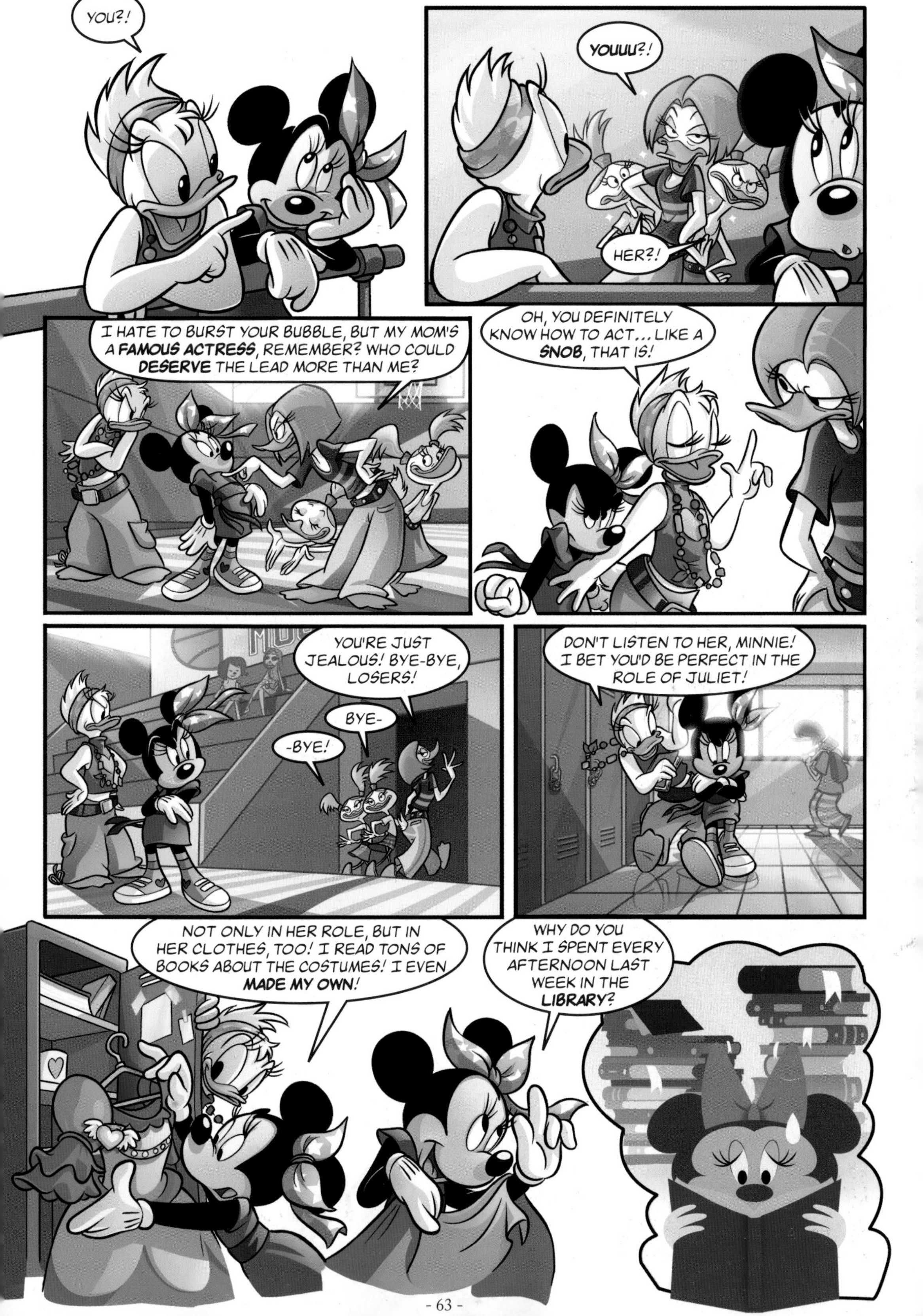

YOU?!
YOUUU?!
HER?!
I HATE TO BURST YOUR BUBBLE, BUT MY MOM'S A FAMOUS ACTRESS, REMEMBER? WHO COULD DESERVE THE LEAD MORE THAN ME?
OH, YOU DEFINITELY KNOW HOW TO ACT... LIKE A SNOB, THAT IS!
YOU'RE JUST JEALOUS! BYE-BYE, LOSERS!
BYE-
-BYE!
DON'T LISTEN TO HER, MINNIE! I BET YOU'D BE PERFECT IN THE ROLE OF JULIET!
NOT ONLY IN HER ROLE, BUT IN HER CLOTHES, TOO! I READ TONS OF BOOKS ABOUT THE COSTUMES! I EVEN MADE MY OWN!
WHY DO YOU THINK I SPENT EVERY AFTERNOON LAST WEEK IN THE LIBRARY?

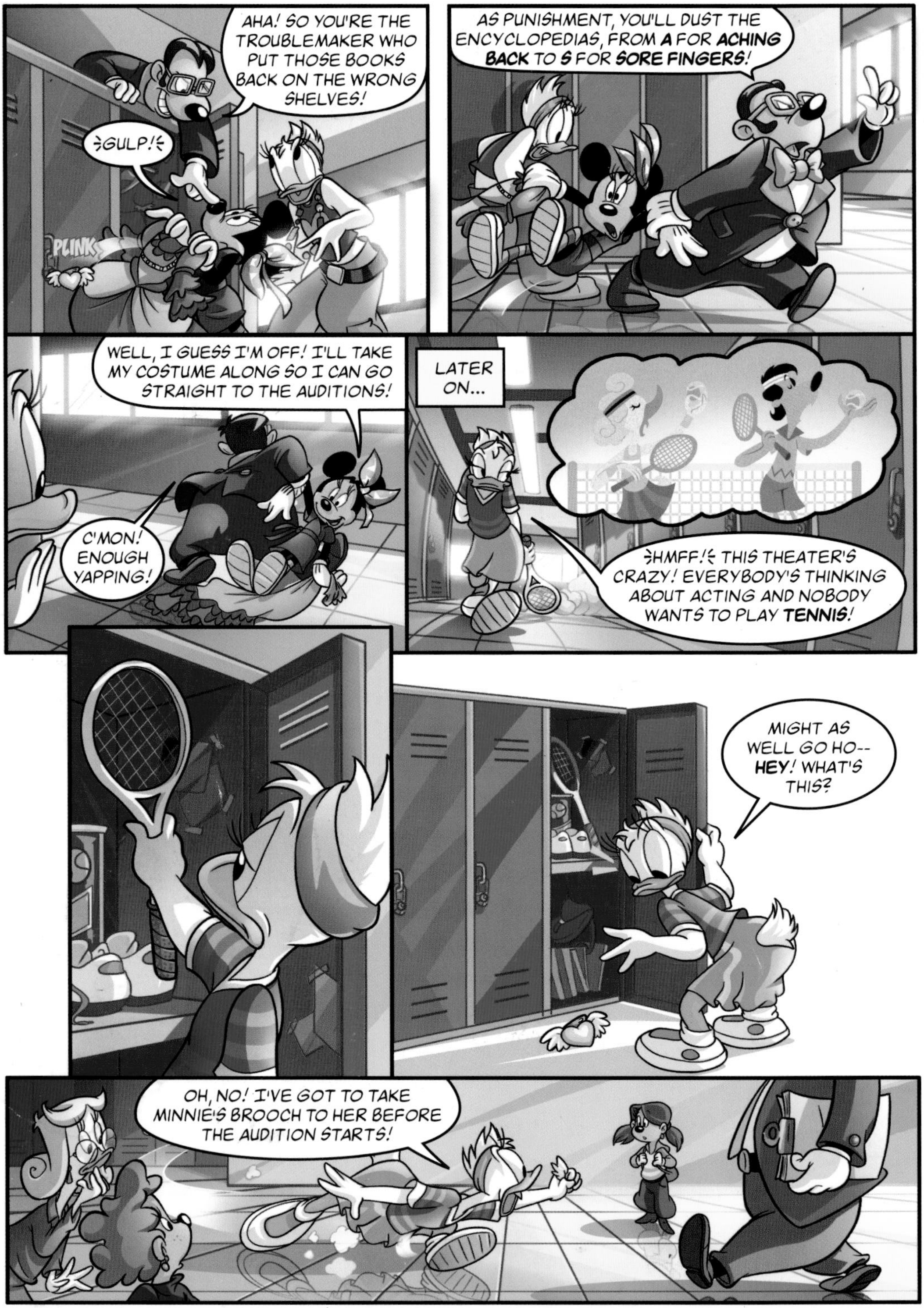
AHA! SO YOU'RE THE TROUBLEMAKER WHO PUT THOSE BOOKS BACK ON THE WRONG SHELVES!
GULP!
PLINK
AS PUNISHMENT, YOU'LL DUST THE ENCYCLOPEDIAS, FROM **A** FOR **ACHING BACK** TO **S** FOR **SORE FINGERS**!
WELL, I GUESS I'M OFF! I'LL TAKE MY COSTUME ALONG SO I CAN GO STRAIGHT TO THE AUDITIONS!
C'MON! ENOUGH YAPPING!
LATER ON...
HMFF! THIS THEATER'S CRAZY! EVERYBODY'S THINKING ABOUT ACTING AND NOBODY WANTS TO PLAY **TENNIS**!
MIGHT AS WELL GO HO-- **HEY**! WHAT'S THIS?
OH, NO! I'VE GOT TO TAKE MINNIE'S BROOCH TO HER BEFORE THE AUDITION STARTS!